"These then, be my men, father; and together we shall fare forth upon the highways and into the by-ways of England to collect from the rich that living which you have ever taught me was owing us."

" 'Tis well, my son, and even as I myself would have it; together we shall ride out, and where we ride a trail of blood shall mark our way.

"From now, henceforth, the name and fame of Norman of Torn shall grow in the land, until even the King shall tremble when he hears it, and shall hate and loathe ye as I have even taught ye to hate and loathe him.

"All England shall curse ye and the blood of Saxon and Norman shall never dry upon your blade."

Such was the heritage of the fearless youth who became known throughout Medieval England as The Outlaw of Torn. But who he really was, how he fared, and how his sword won him the way to his true birthright is a fast-moving novel worthy of Edgar Rice Burroughs, master of adventure.

EDGAR RICE BURROUGHS
1875–1950

One of Chicago's most famous sons was Edgar Rice Burroughs. Young Burroughs tried his hand at many businesses without success, until, at the age of thirty-five, he turned to writing. With the publication of *Tarzan of the Apes* and *A Princess of Mars,* his career was assured. The gratitude of a multitude of readers who found in his imagination exactly the kind of escape reading they loved assured him of a large fortune.

Edgar Rice Burroughs died at home in a town bearing the name of his brain child, Tarzana, California. But, to the countless millions who have enjoyed his works, he will live forever.

EDGAR RICE BURROUGHS
THE OUTLAW OF TORN

ace books
A Division of Charter Communications Inc.
1120 Avenue of the Americas
New York, N.Y. 10036

THE OUTLAW OF TORN

COVER PAINTING BY FRANK FRAZETTA

To My Friend
JOSEPH E. BRAY

First Ace printing: *November, 1968*
Second Ace printing: *January, 1973*

Printed in U.S.A.

CHAPTER I

HERE is a story that has lain dormant for seven hundred years. At first it was suppressed by one of the Plantagenet kings of England. Later it was forgotten. I happened to dig it up by accident. The accident being the relationship of my wife's cousin to a certain Father Superior in a very ancient monastery in Europe.

He let me pry about among a quantity of mildewed and musty manuscripts and I came across this. It is very interesting—partially since it is a bit of hitherto unrecorded history, but principally from the fact that it records the story of a most remarkable revenge and the adventurous life of its innocent victim—Richard, the lost prince of England.

In the retelling of it I have left out most of the history. What interested me was the unique character about whom the tale revolves—the visored horseman who—but let us wait until we get to him.

It all happened in the thirteenth century, and while it was happening it shook England from north to south and from east to west; and reached across the channel and shook France. It started, directly, in the London palace of Henry III, and was the result of a quarrel between the King and his powerful brother-in-law, Simon de Montfort, Earl of Leicester.

Never mind the quarrel, that's history, and you can read all about it at your leisure. But on this June day in the year of our Lord 1243, Henry so forgot himself as to very unjustly accuse De Montfort of treason in the presence of a number of the King's gentlemen.

De Montfort paled. He was a tall, handsome man, and when he drew himself to his full height and turned those gray eyes on the victim of his wrath, as he did that day, he was very imposing. A power in England, second only to the King himself, and with the heart of a lion in him, he answered the King as no other man in all England would have dared answer him.

"My Lord King," he cried, "that you be my Lord King alone prevents Simon de Montfort from demanding satisfaction for such a gross insult. That you take advantage of your kingship to say what you would never dare say were you not king, brands me not a traitor, though it does brand you a coward."

Tense silence fell upon the little company of lords and courtiers as these awful words fell from the lips of a subject, addressed to his king. They were horrified, for De Montfort's bold challenge was to them but little short of sacrilege.

Henry, flushing in mortification and anger, rose to

advance upon De Montfort, but suddenly recollecting the power which he represented, he thought better of whatever action he contemplated, and with a haughty sneer turned to his courtiers.

"Come, my gentlemen," he said, "methought that we were to have a turn with the foils this morning. Already it waxeth late. Come, De Fulm! Come, Leybourn!" and the King left the apartment followed by his gentlemen, all of whom had drawn away from the Earl of Leicester when it became apparent that the royal displeasure was strong against him. As the arras fell behind the departing King, De Montfort shrugged his broad shoulders, and turning, left the apartment by another door.

When the King, with his gentlemen, entered the armory he was still smarting from the humiliation of De Montfort's reproaches, and as he laid aside his surcoat and plumed hat to take the foils with De Fulm his eyes alighted on the master of fence, Sir Jules de Vac, who was advancing with the King's foil and helmet. Henry felt in no mood for fencing with De Fulm, who, like the other sycophants that surrounded him, always allowed the King easily to best him in every encounter.

De Vac he knew to be too jealous of his fame as a swordsman to permit himself to be overcome by aught but superior skill, and this day Henry felt that he could best the devil himself.

The armory was a great room on the main floor of the palace, off the guard room. It was built in a small wing of the building so that it had light from three sides. In charge of it was the lean, grizzled, leatherskinned Sir Jules de Vac, and it was he whom Henry commanded to face him in mimic combat with the foils, for the King wished to go with hammer and tongs at someone to vent his suppressed rage.

So he let De Vac assume to his mind's eye the person of the hated De Montfort, and it followed that De Vac was nearly surprised into an early and mortifying defeat by the King's sudden and clever attack.

Henry III had always been accounted a good swordsman, but that day he quite outdid himself, and in his imagination was about to run the pseudo De Montfort through the heart, to the wild acclaim of his audience. For this fell purpose he had backed the astounded De Vac twice around the hall, when, with a clever feint, and backward step, the master of fence drew the King into the position he wanted him, and with the suddenness of lightning, a little twist of his foil sent Henry's weapon clanging across the floor of the armory.

For an instant the King stood as tense and white as though the hand of death had reached out and touched his heart with its icy fingers. The episode meant more to him than being bested in play by the best swordsman in England—for that surely was no disgrace—to Henry it seemed prophetic of the outcome of a future struggle when he should stand face to face with the real De Montfort; and then, seeing in De Vac only the creature of his imagination with which he had vested the likeness of his powerful brother-in-law, Henry did what he should like to have done to the real Leicester. Drawing off his gauntlet he advanced close to De Vac.

"Dog!" he hissed, and struck the master of fence a

stinging blow across the face, and spat upon him. Then he turned on his heel and strode from the armory.

De Vac had grown old in the service of the kings of England, but he hated all things English and all Englishmen. The dead King John, though hated by all others, he had loved, but with the dead King's bones De Vac's loyalty to the house he served had been buried in the Cathedral of Worcester.

During the years he had served as master of fence at the English Court the sons of royalty had learned to thrust and parry and cut as only De Vac could teach the art; and he had been as conscientious in the discharge of his duties as he had been in his unswerving hatred and contempt for his pupils.

And now the English King had put upon him such an insult as might only be wiped out by blood.

As the blow fell the wiry Frenchman clicked his heels together, and throwing down his foil, he stood erect and rigid as a marble statue before his master. White and livid was his tense drawn face, but he spoke no word.

He might have struck the King, but then there would have been left to him no alternative save death by his own hand; for a king may not fight with a lesser mortal, and he who strikes a king may not live—the king's honor must be satisfied.

Had a French king struck him De Vac would have struck back, and gloried in the fate which permitted him to die for the honor of France; but an English King —pooh! a dog; and who would die for a dog? No, De Vac would find other means of satisfying his wounded pride, he would revel in revenge against this man for whom he felt no loyalty. If possible, he would harm the whole of England if he could, but he would bide his time. He could afford to wait for his opportunity if by waiting he could encompass a more terrible revenge.

De Vac had been born in Paris, the son of a French officer reputed the best swordsman in France. The son had followed closely in the footsteps of his father until, on the latter's death, he could easily claim the title of his sire. How he had left France and entered the service of John of England is not of this story. All the bearing that the life of Jules de Vac has upon the history of England hinges upon but two of his many attributes —his wonderful swordsmanship and his fearful hatred for his adopted country.

CHAPTER II

SOUTH of the armory of Westminster Palace lay the gardens, and here, on the third day following the King's affront to De Vac, might have been a seen a black-haired woman gowned in a violet cyclas, richly embroidered with gold about the yoke and at the bottom of the loose-pointed sleeves, which reached almost to the similar bordering on the lower hem of the garment. A richly wrought leathern girdle, studded with precious stones, and held in place by a huge carved buckle of gold, clasped the garment about her waist so that the upper portion fell outward over the girdle after the manner of a blouse. In the girdle was a long dagger of beautiful workmanship. Dainty sandals encased her feet, while a wimple of violet silk, bordered in gold fringe, lay becomingly over her head and shoulders.

By her side walked a handsome boy of about three, clad, like his companion, in gay colors. His tiny surcoat of scarlet velvet was rich with embroidery, while beneath was a close-fitting tunic of white silk. His doublet was of scarlet, while his long hose of white were cross-gartered with scarlet from his tiny sandals to his knees. On the back of his brown curls sat a flat-brimmed, round-crowned hat in which a single plume of white waved and nodded bravely at each move of the proud little head.

The child's features were well molded, and his frank, bright eyes gave an expression of boyish generosity to a face which otherwise would have been too arrogant and haughty for such a mere baby. As he talked with his companion, little flashes of peremptory authority and dignity, which sat strangely upon one so tiny, caused the young woman at times to turn her head from him that he might not see the smiles which she could scarce repress.

Presently the boy took a ball from his tunic, and, pointing at a little bush near them, said, "Stand you there, Lady Maud, by yonder bush, I would play at toss."

The young woman did as she was bid, and when she had taken her place and turned to face him the boy threw the ball to her. Thus they played beneath the windows of the armory, the boy running blithely after the ball when he missed it, and laughing and shouting in happy glee when he made a particularly good catch.

In one of the windows of the armory overlooking the garden stood a grim, gray, old man, leaning upon his folded arms, his brows drawn together in a malignant scowl, the corners of his mouth set in a stern, cold line.

He looked upon the garden and the playing child, and upon the lovely young woman beneath him, but with eyes which did not see, for De Vac was working out a great problem, the greatest of all his life.

For three days the old man had brooded over his grievance, seeking for some means to be revenged upon the King for the insult which Henry had put upon him. Many schemes had presented themselves to his shrewd and cunning mind, but so far all had been rejected as unworthy of the terrible satisfaction which his wounded pride demanded.

His fancies had for the most part revolved about the unsettled political conditions of Henry's reign, for from these he felt he might wrest that opportunity which could be turned to his own personal uses and to the harm, and possibly the undoing, of the King.

For years an inmate of the palace, and often a listener in the armory when the King played at sword with his friends and favorites, De Vac had heard much which passed between Henry III and his intimates that could well be turned to the King's harm by a shrewd and resourceful enemy.

With all England he knew the utter contempt in which Henry held the terms of the Magna Charta which he so often violated along with his kingly oath to maintain it. But what all England did not know De Vac had gleaned from scraps of conversation dropped in the armory: that Henry was even now negotiating with the leaders of foreign mercenaries, and with Louis IX of France, for a sufficient force of knights and men-at-arms to wage a relentless war upon his own barons that he might effectively put a stop to all future interference by them with the royal prerogative of the Plantagenets to misrule England.

If he could but learn the details of this plan, thought De Vac: the point of landing of the foreign troops; their numbers; the first point of attack. Ah, would it not be sweet revenge indeed to balk the King in this venture so dear to his heart!

A word to De Clare, or De Montfort would bring

the barons and their retainers forty thousand strong to overwhelm the King's forces.

And he would let the King know to whom, and for what cause, he was beholden for his defeat and discomfiture. Possibly the barons would depose Henry, and place a new king upon England's throne, and then De Vac would mock the Plantagenet to his face. Sweet, kind, delectable vengeance, indeed! and the old man licked his thin lips as though to taste the last sweet vestige of some dainty morsel.

And then Chance carried a little leather ball beneath the window where the old man stood; and as the child ran, laughing, to recover it, De Vac's eyes fell upon him, and his former plan for revenge melted as the fog before the noonday sun; and in its stead there opened to him the whole hideous plot of fearsome vengeance as clearly as it were writ upon the leaves of a great book that had been thrown wide before him. And, in so far as he could direct, he varied not one jot from the details of that vividly conceived masterpiece of hellishness during the twenty years which followed.

The little boy who so innocently played in the garden of his royal father was Prince Richard, the three-year-old son of Henry III of England. No published history mentions this little lost prince; only the secret archives of the kings of England tell the story of his strange and adventurous life. His name has been blotted from the records of men; and the revenge of De Vac has passed from the eyes of the world; though in his time it was a real and terrible thing in the hearts of the English.

CHAPTER III

FOR nearly a month the old man haunted the palace, and watched in the gardens for the little Prince until he knew the daily routine of his tiny life with his nurses and governesses.

He saw that when the Lady Maud accompanied him they were wont to repair to the farthermost extremities of the palace grounds where, by a little postern gate, she admitted a certain officer of the Guards to whom the Queen had forbidden the privilege of the court.

There, in a secluded bower, the two lovers whispered their hopes and plans, unmindful of the royal charge playing neglected among the flowers and shrubbery of the garden.

Toward the middle of July De Vac had his plans well laid. He had managed to coax old Brus, the gardener, into letting him have the key to the little postern gate on the plea that he wished to indulge in a midnight escapade, hinting broadly of a fair lady who was to be the partner of his adventure, and, what was more to the point with Brus, at the same time slipping a couple of golden zecchins into the gardener's palm.

Brus, like the other palace servants, considered De Vac a loyal retainer of the house of Plantagenet. Whatever else of mischief De Vac might be up to, Brus was quite sure that in so far as the King was concerned, the key to the postern gate was as safe in De Vac's hands as though Henry himself had it.

The old fellow wondered a little that the morose old master of fence should, at his time in life, indulge in frivolous escapades more befitting the younger sprigs of gentility, but, then, what concern was it of his? Did he not have enough to think about to keep the gardens so that his royal master and mistress might find pleasure in the shaded walks, the well-kept sward, and the gorgeous beds of foliage plants and blooming flowers which he set with such wondrous precision in the formal garden?

Further, two gold zecchins were not often come by so easily as this; and if the dear Lord Jesus saw fit, in his infinite wisdom, to take this means of rewarding his poor servant it ill became such a worm as he to ignore the divine favor. So Brus took the gold zecchins and De Vac the key, and the little prince played happily among the flowers of his royal father's garden, and all were satisfied; which was as it should have been.

That night De Vac took the key to a locksmith on the far side of London; one who could not possibly know him or recognize the key as belonging to the palace. Here he had a duplicate made, waiting impatiently while the old man fashioned it with the crude instruments of his time.

From this little shop De Vac threaded his way through the dirty lanes and alleys of ancient London, lighted at far intervals by an occasional smoky lantern, until he came to a squalid tenement but a short distance from the palace.

A narrow alley ran past the building, ending abruptly at the bank of the Thames in a moldering wooden dock, beneath which the inky waters of the river rose and fell, lapping the decaying piles and surging far beneath the dock to the remote fastnesses inhabited by the great fierce dock rats and their fiercer human antitypes.

Several times De Vac paced the length of this black alley in search of the little doorway of the building he sought. At length he came upon it, and, after repeated pounding with the pommel of his sword, it was opened by a slatternly old hag.

"What would ye of a decent woman at such an ungodly hour?" she grumbled. "Ah, 'tis ye, my Lord?" she added, hastily, as the flickering rays of the candle she bore lighted up De Vac's face. "Welcome, my Lord, thrice welcome. The daughter of the devil welcomes her brother."

"Silence, old hag," cried De Vac. "Is it not enough that you leech me of good merks of such a quantity that you may ever after wear mantles of villosa and feast on simnel bread and malmsey, that you must needs burden me still further with the affliction of thy vile tongue?

"Hast thou the clothes ready bundled and the key, also, to this gate to perdition? And the room: didst set to rights the furnishings I had delivered here, and sweep the century-old accumulation of filth and cobwebs from the floor and rafters? Why, the very air reeked of the dead Romans who builded London twelve hundred years ago. Methinks, too, from the stink, they must have been Roman swineherd who habited this sty with their herds, an' I venture that thou, old sow, hast never touched broom to the place for fear of disturbing the ancient relics of thy kin."

"Cease thy babbling, Lord Satan," cried the woman. "I would rather hear thy money talk than thou, for though it come accursed and tainted from thy rogue hand, yet it speaks with the same sweet and commanding voice as it were fresh from the coffers of the holy church.

"The bundle is ready," she continued, closing the door after De Vac, who had now entered, "and here be the key; but first let us have a payment. I know not what thy foul work may be, but foul it is I know from the secrecy which you have demanded, an' I dare say there will be some who would pay well to learn the whereabouts of the old woman and the child, thy sister and her son you tell me they be, who you are so anxious to hide away in old Til's garret. So it be well for you, my Lord, to pay old Til well and add a few guilders for the peace of her tongue if you would that your prisoner find peace in old Til's house."

"Fetch me the bundle, hag," replied De Vac, "and you shall have gold against a final settlement; more even than we bargained for if all goes well and thou holdest thy vile tongue."

But the old woman's threats had already caused De Vac a feeling of uneasiness, which would have been reflected to an exaggerated degree in the old woman had she known the determination her words had caused in the mind of the old master of fence.

His venture was far too serious, and the results of exposure too fraught with danger, to permit of his taking any chances with a disloyal fellow-conspirator. True, he had not even hinted at the enormity of the plot in which he was involving the old woman, but, as she had said, his stern commands for secrecy had told enough to arouse her suspicions, and with them her curiosity and cupidity. So it was that old Til might well have quailed in her tattered sandals had she but even vaguely guessed the thoughts which passed in De Vac's mind; but the extra gold pieces he dropped into her withered palm as she delivered the bundle to him, together with the promise of more, quite effectually won her loyalty and her silence for the time being.

Slipping the key into the pocket of his tunic and covering the bundle with his long surcoat, De Vac stepped out into the darkness of the alley and hastened toward the dock.

Beneath the planks he found a skiff which he had moored there earlier in the evening, and underneath one of the thwarts he hid the bundle. Then, casting off, he rowed slowly up the Thames until, below the palace walls, he moored near to the little postern gate which let into the lower end of the garden.

Hiding the skiff as best he could in some tangled bushes which grew to the water's edge, set there by order of the King to add to the beauty of the aspect from the river side, De Vac crept warily to the postern and, unchallenged, entered and sought his apartments in the palace.

The next day he returned the original key to Brus, telling the old man that he had not used it after all, since mature reflection had convinced him of the folly of his contemplated adventure, especially in one whose youth was past, and in whose joints the night damp of the Thames might find lodgement for rheumatism.

"Ha, Sir Jules," laughed the old gardener, "Virtue and Vice be twin sisters who come running to do the bidding of the same father, Desire. Were there no desire there would be no virtue, and because one man desires what another does not, who shall say whether the child of his desire be vice or virtue? Or on the other hand if my friend desires his own wife and if that be virtue, then if I also desire his wife, is not that likewise virtue, since we desire the same thing? But if to obtain our desire it be necessary to expose our joints to the Thames' fog then it were virtue to remain at home."

"Right you sound, old mole," said De Vac, smiling, "would that I might learn to reason by your wondrous logic; methinks it might stand me in good stead before I be much older."

"The best sword arm in all Christendom needs no other logic than the sword, I should think," said Brus, returning to his work.

That afternoon De Vac stood in a window of the armory looking out upon the beautiful garden which spread before him to the river wall two hundred yards away. In the foreground were box-bordered walks, smooth, sleek lawns, and formal beds of gorgeous flowering plants, while here and there marble statues of wood nymph and satyr gleamed, sparkling in the brilliant sunlight, or, half shaded by an overhanging bush, took on a semblance of life from the riotous play of light and shadow as the leaves above them moved to and fro in the faint breeze. Farther in the distance the river wall was hidden by more closely massed bushes, and the formal, geometric precision of the nearer view was relieved by a background of vine-colored bowers, and a profusion of small trees and flowering shrubs arranged in studied disorder.

Through this seeming jungle ran tortuous paths, and the carved stone benches of the open garden gave place to rustic seats, and swings suspended from the branches of fruit trees.

Toward this enchanting spot slowly were walking the Lady Maud and her little charge, Prince Richard; all ignorant of the malicious watcher in the window behind them.

A great peacock strutted proudly across the walk before them, and, as Richard ran, childlike, after it, Lady Maud hastened on to the little postern gate which she quickly unlocked admitting her lover who had been waiting without. Relocking the gate the two strolled arm in arm to the little bower which was their trysting place.

As the lovers talked, all self-engrossed, the little Prince played happily about among the trees and flowers, and none saw the stern, determined face which peered through the foliage at a little distance from the playing boy.

Richard was devoting his royal energies to chasing an elusive butterfly which fate led nearer and nearer to the cold, hard watcher in the bushes. Closer and closer came the little Prince, and in another moment he had burst through the flowering shrubs, and stood facing the implacable master of fence.

"Your Highness," said De Vac, bowing to the little fellow, "let old De Vac help you catch the pretty insect."

Richard, having often seen De Vac, did not fear him, and so together they started in pursuit of the butterfly which by now had passed out of sight. De Vac turned their steps toward the little postern gate, but when he would have passed through with the tiny Prince the latter rebelled.

"Come, My Lord Prince," urged De Vac, "methinks the butterfly did but alight without the wall, we can have it and return within the garden in an instant."

"Go thyself and fetch it," replied the Prince; "the King, my father, has forbid me stepping without the palace grounds."

"Come," commanded De Vac, more sternly, "no harm can come to you."

But the child hung back and would not go with him so that De Vac was forced to grasp him roughly by the arm. There was a cry of rage and alarm from the royal child.

"Unhand me, sirrah," screamed the boy. "How dare you lay hands on a prince of England?"

De Vac clapped his hand over the child's mouth to still his cries, but it was too late, the Lady Maud and her lover had heard, and in an instant they were rushing toward the postern gate, the officer drawing his sword as he ran.

When they reached the wall De Vac and the Prince were upon the outside, and the Frenchman had closed and was endeavoring to lock the gate. But handicapped by the struggling boy he had not time to turn the key before the officer threw himself against the panels and burst out before the master of fence, closely followed by the Lady Maud.

De Vac dropped the key and, still grasping the now thoroughly affrighted Prince with his left hand, drew his sword and confronted the officer.

There were no words, there was no need of words; De Vac's intentions were too plain to necessitate any parley, so the two fell upon each other with grim fury; the brave officer facing the best swordsman that France had ever produced in a futile attempt to rescue his young prince.

In a moment De Vac had disarmed him, but, contrary to the laws of chivalry, he did not lower his point until it had first plunged through the heart of his brave antagonist. Then with a bound he leaped between Lady Maud and the gate, so that she could not retreat into the garden and give the alarm.

Still grasping the trembling child in his iron grip he stood facing the lady in waiting, his back against the door.

"*Mon Dieu,* Sir Jules," she cried, "hast thou gone mad?"

"No, My Lady," he answered, "but I had not thought to do the work which now lies before me. Why didst thou not keep a still tongue in thy head and let his patron saint look after the welfare of this princeling? Your rashness has brought you to a pretty pass, for it must be either you or I, My Lady, and it cannot be I. Say thy prayers and compose thyself for death."

Henry III, King of England, sat in his council chamber surrounded by the great lords and nobles who composed his suit. He awaited Simon de Montfort, Earl of Leicester, whom he had summoned that he might heap still further indignities upon him with the intention of degrading and humiliating him that he might leave England forever. The King feared this mighty kinsman who so boldly advised him against the weak follies which were bringing his kingdom to a condition of revolution.

What the outcome of this audience would have been none may say, for Leicester had but just entered and saluted his sovereign when there came an interruption which drowned the petty wrangles of king and courtier in a common affliction that touched the hearts of all.

There was a commotion at one side of the room, the arras parted, and Eleanor, Queen of England, staggered toward the throne, tears streaming down her pale cheeks.

"Oh, My Lord! My Lord!" she cried, "Richard our son, has been assassinated and thrown into the Thames."

In an instant all was confusion and turmoil, and it was with the greatest difficulty that the King finally obtained a coherent statement from his queen.

It seemed that when the Lady Maud had not returned to the palace with Prince Richard at the proper time, the Queen had been notified and an immediate search had been instituted—a search which did not end for over twenty years; but the first fruits of it turned the hearts of the court to stone, for there beside the open postern gate lay the dead bodies of Lady Maud and a certain officer of the Guards, but nowhere was there a sign or trace of Prince Richard, second son of Henry III of England, and at that time the youngest prince of the realm.

It was two days before the absence of De Vac was noted, and then it was that one of the lords in waiting to the King reminded his majesty of the episode of the fencing bout, and a motive for the abduction of the King's little son became apparent.

An edict was issued requiring the examination of every child in England, for on the left breast of the little Prince was a birthmark which closely resembled a lily, and when after a year no child was found bearing such a mark and no trace of De Vac uncovered, the search was carried into France, nor was it ever wholly relinquished at any time for more than twenty years.

The first theory, of assassination, was quickly abandoned when it was subjected to the light of reason, for it was evident that an assassin could have dispatched the little Prince at the same time that he killed the Lady Maud and her lover, had such been his desire.

The most eager factor in the search for Prince Richard was Simon de Montfort, Earl of Leicester, whose affection for his royal nephew had always been so marked as to have been commented upon by the members of the King's household.

Thus for a time the rupture between De Montfort

and his king was healed, and although the great noble-man was divested of his authority in Gascony he suf-fered little further oppression at the hands of his royal master.

CHAPTER IV

AS De Vac drew his sword from the heart of the Lady
Maud he winced, for, merciless though he was, he had
shrunk from this cruel task. Too far he had gone, however, to back down now, and, had he left the Lady
Maud alive, the whole of the palace guard and all the
city of London would have been on his heels in ten
minutes; there would have been no escape.

The little Prince was now so terrified that he could
but tremble and whimper in his fright. So fearful was
he of the terrible De Vac that a threat of death easily
stilled his tongue, and so the grim, old man led him to
the boat hidden deep in the dense bushes.

De Vac did not dare remain in this retreat until dark,
as he had first intended. Instead he drew a dingy,
ragged dress from the bundle beneath the thwart and
in this disguised himself as an old woman, drawing a
cotton wimple low over his head and forehead to hide
his short hair. Concealing the child beneath the other
articles of clothing he pushed off from the bank, and,
rowing close to the shore, hastened down the Thames
toward the old dock where, the previous night, he had
concealed his skiff. He reached his destination unno-
ticed, and, running in beneath the dock, worked the
boat far into the dark recess of the cave-like retreat.

Here he determined to hide until darkness had fallen,
for he knew that the search would be on for the little
lost Prince at any moment, and that none might traverse

the streets of London without being subject to the closest scrutiny.

Taking advantage of the forced wait De Vac undressed the Prince and clothed him in other garments, which had been wrapped in the bundle hidden beneath the thwart; a little red cotton tunic with hose to match, a black doublet and a tiny leather jerkin and leather cap.

The discarded clothing of the Prince he wrapped about a huge stone torn from the disintegrating masonry of the river wall, and consigned the bundle to the voiceless river.

The Prince had by now regained some of his former assurance, and, finding that De Vac seemed not to intend harming him, the little fellow commenced questioning his grim companion, his childish wonder at this strange adventure getting the better of his former apprehension.

"What do we here, Sir Jules?" he asked. "Take me back to the King's, my father's palace. I like not this dark hole nor the strange garments you have placed upon me."

"Silence, boy!" commanded the old man. "Sir Jules be dead, nor are you a king's son. Remember these two things well, nor ever again let me hear you speak the name Sir Jules, or call yourself a prince."

The boy went silent, again cowed by the fierce tone of his captor. Presently he began to whimper, for he was tired and hungry and frightened—just a poor little baby, helpless and hopeless in the hands of this cruel enemy, all his royalty as nothing, all gone with the silken finery which lay in the thick mud at the bottom of the Thames—and presently he dropped into a fitful sleep in the bottom of the skiff.

When darkness had settled, De Vac pushed the skiff outward to the side of the dock and gathering the sleeping child in his arms stood listening, preparatory to mounting to the alley which led to old Til's place.

As he stood thus a faint sound of clanking armor came to his attentive ears; louder and louder it grew until there could be no doubt but that a number of men were approaching.

De Vac resumed his place in the skiff, and again drew it far beneath the dock. Scarcely had he done so ere a party of armored knights and men-at-arms clanked out upon the planks above him from the mouth of the dark alley. Here they stopped as though for consultation and plainly could the listener below hear every word of their conversation.

"De Montfort," said one, "what thinkest thou of it? Can it be that the Queen is right and that Richard lies dead beneath these black waters?"

"No, De Clare," replied a deep voice, which De Vac recognized as that of the Earl of Leicester. "The hand that could steal the Prince from out of the very gardens of his sire without the knowledge of Lady Maud or her companion, which must evidently have been the case, could more easily and safely have dispatched him within the gardens had that been the object of this strange attack. I think, My Lord, that presently we shall hear from some bold adventurer who holds the little Prince for ransom. God give that such may be the case, for of all the winsome and affectionate little fellows I have ever seen, not even excepting mine own dear son, the little Richard was the most to be beloved. Would that I might get my hands upon the foul devil who has done this horrid deed."

Beneath the planks, not four feet from where Leicester stood, lay the object of his search. The clanking armor, the heavy spurred feet, and the voices above him had awakened the little Prince and with a startled cry he sat upright in the bottom of the skiff. Instantly De Vac's iron hand clapped over the tiny mouth, but not before a single faint wail had reached the ears of the men above.

"Hark! What was that, My Lord?" cried one of the men-at-arms.

In tense silence they listened for a repetition of the sound and then De Montfort cried out:

"What ho, below there! Who is it beneath the dock? Answer, in the name of the King!"

Richard, recognizing the voice of his favorite uncle, struggled to free himself, but De Vac's ruthless hand crushed out the weak efforts of the babe, and all was quiet as the tomb, while those above stood listening for a repetition of the sound.

"Dock rats," said De Clare, and then as though the devil guided them to protect his own, two huge rats scurried upward from between the loose boards, and ran squealing up the dark alley.

"Right you are," said De Montfort, "but I could have sworn 'twas a child's feeble wail had I not seen the two filthy rodents with mine own eyes. Come, let us to the next vile alley. We have met with no success here, though that old hag who called herself Til seemed overanxious to bargain for the future information she seemed hopeful of being able to give us."

As they moved off, their voices grew fainter in the ears of the listeners beneath the dock and soon were lost in the distance.

"A close shave," thought De Vac, as he again took up the child and prepared to gain the dock. No further noises occurring to frighten him he soon reached the door to Til's house and inserting the key crept noiselessly to the garret toom which he had rented from his ill-favored hostess.

There were no stairs from the upper floor to the garret above, this ascent being made by means of a wooden ladder which De Vac pulled up after him, closing and securing the aperture, through which he climbed with his burden, by means of a heavy trapdoor equipped with thick bars.

The apartment which they now entered extended across the entire east end of the building, and had windows upon three sides. These were heavily curtained. The apartment was lighted by a small cresset hanging from a rafter near the center of the room.

The walls were unplastered and the rafters unceiled; the whole bearing a most barnlike and unhospitable appearance.

In one corner was a huge bed, and across the room a smaller cot; a cupboard, a table, and two benches completed the furnishings. These articles De Vac had purchased for the room against the time when he should occupy it with his little prisoner.

On the table were a loaf of black bread, an earthenware jar containing honey, a pitcher of milk and two drinking horns. To these De Vac immediately gave his attention, commanding the child to partake of what he wished.

Hunger for the moment overcame the little Prince's fears, and he set to with avidity upon the strange, rough fare, made doubly coarse by the rude utensils and the bare surroundings, so unlike the royal magnificence of his palace apartments.

While the child ate, De Vac hastened to the lower floor of the building in search of Til whom he now thoroughly mistrusted and feared. The words of De Montfort, which he had overheard at the dock, convinced him that here was one more obstacle to the fulfillment of his revenge which must be removed as had the Lady Maud; but in this instance there was neither youth nor beauty to plead the cause of the intended victim, or to cause the grim executioner a pang of remorse.

When he found the old hag she was already dressed to go upon the street, in fact he intercepted her at the very door of the building. Still clad as he was in the mantle and wimple of an old woman, Til did not, at first, recognize him, and when he spoke she burst into a nervous, cackling laugh, as one caught in the perpetration of some questionable act, nor did her manner escape the shrewd notice of the wily master of fence.

"Whither, old hag?" he asked.

"To visit Mag Tunk at the alley's end, by the river, My Lord," she replied, with more respect than she had been wont to accord him.

"Then I will accompany you part way, my friend, and, perchance, you can give me a hand with some packages I left behind me in the skiff I have moored there."

And so the two walked together through the dark alley to the end of the rickety, dismantled dock; the one thinking of the vast reward the King would lavish upon her for the information she felt sure she alone could give; the other feeling beneath his mantle for the hilt of a long dagger which nestled there.

As they reached the water's edge De Vac was walking with his right shoulder behind his companion's left, in his hand was gripped the keen blade and as the woman halted on the dock the point that hovered just below her left shoulder-blade plunged, soundless, into her heart at the same instant that De Vac's left hand swung up and grasped her throat in a grip of steel.

There was no sound, barely a struggle of the convulsively stiffening old muscles, and then, with a push from De Vac, the body lunged forward into the Thames, where a dull splash marked the end of the last hope that Prince Richard might be rescued from the clutches of his Nemesis.

CHAPTER V

FOR three years following the disappearance of Prince Richard a bent old woman lived in the heart of London within a stone's throw of the King's palace. In a small back room she lived, high up in the attic of an old building, and with her was a little boy who never went abroad alone, nor by day. And upon his left breast was a strange mark which resembled a lily. When the bent old woman was safely in her attic room, with bolted door behind her, she was wont to straighten up, and discard her dingy mantle for more comfortable and becoming doublet and hose.

For years she worked assiduously with the little boy's education. There were three subjects in her curriculum; French, swordsmanship and hatred of all things English, especially the reigning house of England.

The old woman had had made a tiny foil and had commenced teaching the little boy the art of fence when he was but three years old.

"You will be the greatest swordsman in the world when you are twenty, my son," she was wont to say, "and then you shall go out and kill many Englishmen. Your name shall be hated and cursed the length and breadth of England, and when you finally stand with the halter about your neck—a—ha, then will I speak. Then shall they know."

The little boy did not understand it all, he only knew that he was comfortable, and had warm clothing, and

34

all he required to eat, and that he would be a great man when he learned to fight with a real sword, and had grown large enough to wield one. He also knew that he hated Englishmen, but why, he did not know.

Way back in the uttermost recesses of his little, childish head he seemed to remember a time when his life and surroundings had been very different; when, instead of this old woman, there had been many people around him, and a sweet faced woman had held him in her arms and kissed him, before he was taken off to bed at night; but he could not be sure, maybe it was only a dream he remembered, for he dreamed many strange and wonderful dreams.

When the little boy was about six years of age a strange man came to their attic home to visit the little old woman. It was in the dusk of the evening but the old woman did not light the cresset, and further, she whispered to the little boy to remain in the shadows of a far corner of the bare chamber.

The stranger was old and bent and had a great beard which hid almost his entire face except for two piercing eyes, a great nose and a bit of wrinkled forehead. When he spoke he accompanied his words with many shrugs of his narrow shoulders and with waving of his arms and other strange and amusing gesticulations. The child was fascinated. Here was the first amusement of his little starved life. He listened intently to the conversation, which was in French.

"I have just the thing for madame," the stranger was saying. "It be a noble and stately hall far from the beaten way. It was built in the old days by Harold the

Saxon, but in later times death and poverty and the disfavor of the King have wrested it from his descendants. A few years since Henry granted it to that spendthrift favorite of his, Henri de Macy, who pledged it to me for a sum he hath been unable to repay. Today it be my property, and as it be far from Paris you may have it for the mere song I have named. It be a wondrous bargain, madame."

"And when I come upon it I shall find that I have bought a crumbling pile of ruined masonry, unfit to house a family of foxes," replied the old woman peevishly.

"One tower hath fallen, and the roof for half the length of one wing hath sagged and tumbled in," explained the old Frenchman. "But the three lower stories be intact and quite habitable. It be much grander even now than the castles of many of England's noble barons, and the price, madame—ah, the price be so ridiculously low."

Still the old woman hesitated.

"Come," said the Frenchman, "I have it. Deposit the money with Isaac the Jew—thou knowest him?—and he shall hold it together with the deed for forty days, which will give thee ample time to travel to Derby and inspect thy purchase. If thou be not entirely satisfied Isaac the Jew shall return thy money to thee and the deed to me, but if at the end of forty days thou hast not made demand for thy money then shall Isaac send the deed to thee and the money to me. Be not this an easy and fair way out of the difficulty?"

The little old woman thought for a moment and at

last conceded that it seemed quite a fair way to arrange the matter. And thus it was accomplished.

Several days later the little old woman called the child to her.

"We start tonight upon a long journey to our new home. Thy face shall be wrapped in many rags, for thou hast a most grievous toothache. Dost understand?"

"But I have no toothache. My teeth do not pain me at all. I—" expostulated the child.

"Tut, tut," interrupted the little old woman. "Thou *hast* a toothache, and so thy face must be wrapped in many rags. And listen, should any ask thee upon the way why thy face be so wrapped thou art to *say* that thou hast a toothache. And thou do not do as I say the King's men will take us and we shall be hanged, for the King hateth us. If thou hatest the English King and lovest thy life do as I command."

"I hate the King," replied the little boy. "For this reason I shall do as thou sayest."

So it was that they set out that night upon their long journey north toward the hills of Derby. For many days they travelled, riding upon two small donkeys. Strange sights filled the days for the little boy who remembered nothing outside the bare attic of his London home and the dirty London alleys that he had traversed only by night.

They wound across beautiful parklike meadows and through dark, forbidding forests, and now and again they passed tiny hamlets of thatched huts. Occasionally they saw armored knights upon the highway, alone or in small parties, but the child's companion always managed to hasten into cover at the road side until the grim riders had passed.

Once, as they lay in hiding in a dense wood beside a little open glade across which the road wound, the boy saw two knights enter the glade from either side. For a moment they drew rein and eyed each other in silence, and then one, a great black mailed knight upon a black charger, cried out something to the other which the boy could not catch. The other knight made no response other than to rest his lance upon his thigh and with lowered point ride toward his ebon adversary. For a dozen paces their great steeds trotted slowly toward one another but presently the knights urged them into full gallop, and when the two iron men on their iron trapped chargers came together in the center of the glade it was with all the terrific impact of full charge.

The lance of the black knight smote full upon the linden shield of his foeman, the staggering weight of the mighty black charger hurtled upon the gray who went down with his rider into the dust of the highway. The momentum of the black carried him fifty paces beyond the fallen horseman before his rider could rein him in, then the black knight turned to view the havoc he had wrought. The gray horse was just staggering dizzily to his feet, but his mailed rider lay quiet and still where he had fallen.

With raised visor the black knight rode back to the side of his vanquished foe. There was a cruel smile upon his lips as he leaned toward the prostrate form. He spoke tauntingly, but there was no response, then he prodded the fallen man with the point of his spear.

Even this elicited no movement. With a shrug of his iron clad shoulders the black knight wheeled and rode on down the road until he had disappeared from sight within the gloomy shadows of the encircling forest.

The little boy was spell-bound. Naught like this had he ever seen or dreamed.

"Some day thou shalt go and do likewise, my son," said the little old woman.

"Shall I be clothed in armor and ride upon a great black steed?" he asked.

"Yes, and thou shalt ride the highways of England with thy stout lance and mighty sword, and behind thee thou shalt leave a trail of blood and death, for every man shalt be thy enemy. But come, we must be on our way."

They rode on leaving the dead knight where he had fallen, but always in his memory the child carried the thing that he had seen, longing for the day when he should be great and strong like the formidable black knight.

On another day as they were hiding in a deserted hovel to escape the notice of a caravan of merchants journeying up-country with their wares, they saw a band of ruffians rush out from the concealing shelter of some bushes at the far side of the highway and fall upon the surprised and defenseless tradesmen.

Ragged, bearded, uncouth villains they were, armed mostly with bludgeons and daggers, with here and there a cross-bow. Without mercy they attacked the old and the young, beating them down in cold blood even when they offered no resistance. Those of the caravan who could escaped, the balance the highwaymen left dead or dying in the road, as they hurried away with their loot.

At first the child was horror-struck, but when he turned to the little old woman for sympathy he found a grim smile upon her thin lips. She noted his expression of dismay.

"It is naught, my son. But English curs setting upon English swine. Some day thou shalt set upon both—they be only fit for killing."

The boy made no reply, but he thought a great deal about that which he had seen. Knights were cruel to knights—the poor were cruel to the rich—and every day of the journey had forced upon his childish mind that everyone must be very cruel and hard upon the poor. He had seen them in all their sorrow and misery and poverty—stretching a long, scattering line all the way from London town. Their bent backs, their poor thin bodies and their hopeless, sorrowful faces attesting the weary wretchedness of their existence.

"Be no one happy in all the world?" he once broke out to the old woman.

"Only he who wields the mightiest sword," responded the old woman. "You have seen, my son, that all Englishmen are beasts. They set upon and kill one another for little provocation or for no provocation at all. When thou shalt be older thou shalt go forth and kill them all, for unless thou kill them they will kill thee."

At length, after tiresome days upon the road, they came to a little hamlet in the hills. Here the donkeys were disposed of and a great horse purchased, upon which the two rode far up into a rough and uninviting country away from the beaten track, until late one evening they approached a ruined castle.

The frowning walls towered high against the moonlit sky beyond, and where a portion of the roof had fallen in, the cold moon, shining through the narrow unglazed windows, gave to the mighty pile the likeness of a huge, many eyed ogre crouching upon the flank of a deserted world, for nowhere was there other sign of habitation.

Before this somber pile the two dismounted. The little boy was filled with awe and his childish imagination ran riot as they approached the crumbling barbican on foot, leading the horse after them. From the dark shadows of the ballium they passed into the moonlit inner court. At the far end the old woman found the ancient stables, and here with decaying planks she penned the horse for the night, pouring a measure of oats upon the floor for him from a bag which had hung across his rump.

Then she led the way into the dense shadows of the castle, lighting their advance with a flickering pine knot. The old planking of the floors, long unused, groaned and rattled beneath their approach. There was a sudden scamper of clawed feet before them, and a red fox dashed by in a frenzy of alarm toward the freedom of the outer night.

Presently they came to the great hall. The old woman pushed open the great doors upon their creaking hinges and lit up dimly the mighty, cavernous interior with the puny rays of their feeble torch. As they stepped cautiously within an impalpable dust arose in little spurts from the long rotted rushes that crumbled beneath their feet. A huge bat circled wildly with loud fluttering wings in evident remonstrance at this rude intrusion. Strange creatures of the night scurried or wriggled across wall and floor.

But the child was unafraid. Fear had not been a part of the old woman's curriculum. The boy did not know the meaning of the word, nor was he ever in his after life to experience the sensation. With childish eagerness he followed his companion as she inspected the interior of the chamber. It was still an imposing room. The boy clapped his hands in delight at the beauties of the carved and panelled walls and the oak beamed ceiling, stained almost black from the smoke of torches and oil cressets that had lighted it in bygone days, aided, no doubt, by the wood fires which had burned in its two immense fireplaces to cheer the merry throng of noble revellers that had so often sat about the great table into the morning hours.

Here they took up their abode. But the bent, old woman was no longer an old woman—she had become a straight, wiry, active old man.

The little boy's education went on—French, swordsmanship and hatred of the English—the same thing year after year with the addition of horsemanship after he was ten years old. At this time the old man commenced teaching him to speak English, but with a studied and very marked French accent. During all his life now he could not remember of having spoken to any living being other than his guardian, whom he had

42

been taught to address as father. Nor did the boy have any name—he was just "my son."

His life in the Derby hills was so filled with the hard, exacting duties of his education that he had little time to think of the strange loneliness of his existence; nor is it probable that he missed that companionship of others of his own age of which, never having had experience in it, he could scarce be expected to regret or yearn for.

At fifteen the youth was a magnificent swordsman and horseman, and with an utter contempt for pain or danger—a contempt which was the result of the heroic methods adopted by the little old man in the training of him. Often the two practiced with razor-sharp swords, and without armor or other protection of any description.

"Thus only," the old man was wont to say, "mayst thou become the absolute master of thy blade. Of such a nicety must be thy handling of the weapon that thou mayst touch an antagonist at will, and so lightly, shouldst thou desire, that thy point, wholly under the control of a master hand, mayst be stopped before it inflicts so much as a scratch."

But in practice there were many accidents, and then one or both of them would nurse a punctured skin for a few days. So, while blood was often let on both sides, the training produced a fearless swordsman who was so truly the master of his point that he could stop a thrust within a fraction of an inch of the spot he sought.

At fifteen he was a very strong and straight and

handsome lad. Bronzed and hardy from his outdoor life; of few words, for there was none that he might talk with save the taciturn old man; hating the English, for that he was taught as thoroughly as swordsmanship; speaking French fluently and English poorly—and waiting impatiently for the day when the old man should send him out into the world with clanking armor and lance and shield to do battle with the knights of England.

It was about this time that there occurred the first important break in the monotony of his existence. Far down the rocky trail that led from the valley below through the Derby hills to the ruined castle, three armored knights urged their tired horses late one afternoon of a chill autumn day. Off the main road and far from any habitation, they had espied the castle's towers through a rift in the hills, and now they spurred toward it in search of food and shelter.

As the road led them winding higher into the hills they suddenly emerged upon the downs below the castle where a sight met their eyes which caused them to draw rein and watch in admiration. There before them upon the downs a boy battled with a lunging, rearing horse—a perfect demon of a black horse. Striking and biting in a frenzy of rage it sought ever to escape or injure the lithe figure which clung leech-like to its shoulder.

The boy was on the ground. His left hand grasped the heavy mane; his right arm lay across the beast's withers and his right hand drew steadily in upon a halter rope with which he had taken a half hitch about the horse's muzzle. Now the black reared and wheeled, striking and biting, full upon the youth, but the active figure swung with him—always just behind the giant shoulder—and ever and ever he drew the great arched neck farther and farther to the right.

As the animal plunged hither and thither in great leaps he dragged the boy with him, but all his mighty efforts were unavailing to loosen the grip upon mane and withers. Suddenly he reared straight into the air carrying the youth with him, then with a vicious lunge he threw himself backward upon the ground.

"It's death!" exclaimed one of the knights, "he will kill the youth yet, Beauchamp."

"No!" cried he addressed. "Look! He is up again and the boy still clings as tightly to him as his own black hide."

" 'Tis true," exclaimed another, "but he hath lost what he had gained upon the halter—he must needs fight it all out again from the beginning."

And so the battle went on again as before, the boy again drawing the iron neck slowly to the right—the beast fighting and squealing as though possessed of a thousand devils. A dozen times as the head bent farther and farther toward him the boy loosed his hold upon the mane and reached quickly down to grasp the near fore pastern. A dozen times the horse shook off the new hold, but at length the boy was successful, and the knee was bent and the hoof drawn up to the elbow.

Now the black fought at a disadvantage, for he was on but three feet and his neck was drawn about in an awkward and unnatural position. His efforts became weaker and weaker. The boy talked incessantly to him in a quiet voice, and there was a shadow of a smile upon his lips. Now he bore heavily upon the black withers pulling the horse toward him. Slowly the beast sank upon his bent knee—pulling backward until his off fore leg was stretched straight before him. Then with a final surge the youth pulled him over upon his side, and as he fell slipped prone beside him. One sinewy hand shot to the rope just beneath the black chin—the other grasped a slim, pointed ear.

For a few minutes the horse fought and kicked to gain his liberty, but with his head held to the earth he was as powerless in the hands of the boy as a baby would have been. Then he sank panting and exhausted into mute surrender.

"Well done!" cried one of the knights. "Simon de Montfort himself never mastered a horse in better order, my boy. Who be thou?"

In an instant the lad was upon his feet his eyes searching for the speaker. The horse, released, sprang up also, and the two stood—the handsome boy and the beautiful black—gazing with startled eyes, like two wild things, at the strange intruder who confronted them.

"Come, Sir Mortimer!" cried the boy, and turning he led the prancing but subdued animal toward the castle and through the ruined barbican into the court beyond.

"What ho, there, lad!" shouted Paul of Merely. "We wouldst not harm thee—come, we but ask the way to the castle of De Stutevill."

The three knights listened but there was no answer.

"Come, Sir Knights," spoke Paul of Merely, "we will ride within and learn what manner of churls inhabit this ancient rookery."

As they entered the great courtyard, magnificent even in its ruined grandeur, they were met by a little, grim old man who asked them in no gentle tones what they would of them there.

"We have lost our way in these devilish Derby hills of thine, old man," replied Paul of Merely. "We seek the castle of Sir John de Stutevill."

"Ride down straight to the river road, keeping the first trail to the right, and when thou hast come there turn again to thy right and ride north beside the river—thou canst not miss the way—it be plain as the nose before thy face," and with that the old man turned to enter the castle.

"Hold, old fellow!" cried the spokesman. "It be nigh onto sunset now, and we care not to sleep out again this night as we did the last. We will tarry with you then till morn that we may take up our journey refreshed, upon rested steeds."

The old man grumbled, and it was with poor grace that he took them in to feed and house them over night. But there was nothing else for it, since they would have taken his hospitality by force had he refused to give it voluntarily.

From their guests the two learned something of the conditions outside their Derby hills. The old man showed less interest than he felt, but to the boy, notwithstanding that the names he heard meant nothing to him, it was like unto a fairy tale to hear of the wondrous doings of earl and baron, bishop and king.

"If the King does not mend his ways," said one of the knights, "we will drive his whole accursed pack of foreign blood-suckers into the sea."

"De Montfort has told him as much a dozen times, and now that all of us, both Norman and Saxon barons, have already met together and formed a pact for our mutual protection the King must surely realize that the time for temporizing be past, and that unless he would have a civil war upon his hands he must keep the promises he so glibly makes, instead of breaking them the moment De Montfort's back be turned."

"He fears his brother-in-law," interrupted another of the knights, "even more than the devil fears holy water. I was in attendance on his majesty some weeks since when he was going down the Thames upon the royal barge. We were overtaken by as severe a thunder storm as I have ever seen, of which the King was in such abject fear that he commanded that we land at the Bishop of Durham's palace opposite which we then were. De Montfort, who was residing there, came to meet Henry, with all due respect, observing, 'What do you fear, now, Sire, the tempest has passed?' And what thinkest thou old 'waxen heart' replied? Why, still trembling, he said, 'I do indeed fear thunder and lightning much, but, by the hand of God, I tremble before you more than for all the thunder in Heaven!'"

"I surmise," interjected the grim, old man, "that De Montfort has in some manner gained an ascendancy over the King. Think you he looks so high as the throne itself?"

"Not so," cried the oldest of the knights. "Simon de Montfort works for England's weal alone—and methinks, nay knowest, that he would be first to spring to arms to save the throne for Henry. He but fights the King's rank and covetous advisers, and though he must needs seem to defy the King himself, it be but to save his tottering power from utter collapse. But, gad, how the King hates him. For a time it seemed that there might be a permanent reconciliation when, for years after the disappearance of the little Prince Richard, De Montfort devoted much of his time and private fortune to prosecuting a search through all the world for the little fellow, of whom he was inordinately fond. This self-sacrificing interest on his part won over the King and Queen for many years, but of late his unremitting hostility to their continued extravagant waste of the national resources has again hardened them toward him."

The old man, growing uneasy at the turn the conversation threatened, sent the youth from the room on some pretext, and himself left to prepare supper.

As they were sitting at the evening meal one of the nobles eyed the boy intently, for he was indeed good to look upon; his bright handsome face, clear, intelligent gray eyes, and square strong jaw framed in a mass of brown waving hair banged at the forehead and falling about his ears, where it was again cut square at the sides and back, after the fashion of the times.

His upper body was clothed in a rough under tunic of wool, stained red, over which he wore a short leathern jerkin, while his doublet was also of leather, a soft and finely tanned piece of undressed doeskin. His long hose, fitting his shapely legs as closely as another layer of skin, were of the same red wool as his tunic, while his strong leather sandals were cross-gartered half way to his knees with narrow bands of leather.

A leathern girdle about his waist supported a sword and a dagger and a round skull cap of the same material, to which was fastened a falcon's wing, completed his picturesque and becoming costume.

"Your son?" he asked, turning to the old man.

"Yes," was the growling response.

"He favors you but little, old fellow, except in his cursed French accent.

" 'S blood, Beauchamp," he continued, turning to one of his companions, "an' were he set down in court I wager our gracious Queen would be hard put to it to tell him from the young Prince Edward. Dids't ever see so strange a likeness?"

"Now that you speak of it, My Lord, I see it plainly. It is indeed a marvel," answered Beauchamp.

Had they glanced at the old man during this colloquy they would have seen a blanched face, drawn with inward fear and rage.

Presently the oldest member of the party of three knights spoke in a grave quiet tone.

"And how old might you be, my son?" he asked the boy.

"I do not know."

"And your name?"

"I do not know what you mean. I have no name.

50

My father calls me son and no other ever before addressed me."

At this juncture the old man arose and left the room, saying he would fetch more food from the kitchen, but he turned immediately he had passed the doorway and listened from without.

"The lad appears about fifteen," said Paul of Merely, lowering his voice, "and so would be the little lost Prince Richard, if he lives. This one does not know his name, or his age, yet he looks enough like Prince Edward to be his twin."

"Come, my son," he continued aloud, "open your jerkin and let us have a look at your left breast, we shall read a true answer there."

"Are you Englishmen?" asked the boy without making a move to comply with their demand.

"That we be, my son," said Beauchamp.

"Then it were better that I die than do your bidding, for all Englishmen are pigs and I loathe them as becomes a gentleman of France. I do not uncover my body to the eyes of swine."

The knights, at first taken back by this unexpected outbreak, finally burst into uproarious laughter.

"Indeed," cried Paul of Merely, "spoken as one of the King's foreign favorites might speak, and they ever told the good God's truth. But come lad, we would not harm you—do as I bid."

"No man lives who can harm me while a blade hangs at my side," answered the boy, "and as for doing as you bid, I take orders from no man other than my father."

Beauchamp and Greystoke laughed aloud at the discomfiture of Paul of Merely, but the latter's face hardened in anger, and without further words he strode forward with outstretched hand to tear open the boy's leathern jerkin, but met with the gleaming point of a sword and a quick sharp, "*En garde!*" from the boy.

There was naught for Paul of Merely to do but draw his own weapon, in self-defense, for the sharp point of the boy's sword was flashing in and out against his unprotected body, inflicting painful little jabs, and the boy's tongue was murmuring low-toned taunts and insults as it invited him to draw and defend himself or be stuck "like the English pig you are."

Paul of Merely was a brave man and he liked not the idea of drawing against this stripling, but he argued that he could quickly disarm him without harming the lad, and he certainly did not care to be further humiliated before his comrades.

But when he had drawn and engaged his youthful antagonist he discovered that, far from disarming him, he would have the devil's own job of it to keep from being killed.

Never in all his long years of fighting had he faced such an agile and dexterous enemy, and as they backed this way and that about the room great beads of sweat stood upon the brow of Paul of Merely, for he realized that he was fighting for his life against a superior swordsman.

The loud laughter of Beauchamp and Greystoke soon subsided to grim smiles, and presently they looked on with startled faces in which fear and apprehension were dominant.

The boy was fighting as a cat might play with a mouse. No sign of exertion was apparent, and his haughty confident smile told louder than words that he had in no sense let himself out to his full capacity.

Around and around the room they circled, the boy always advancing, Paul of Merely always retreating. The din of their clashing swords and the heavy breathing of the older man were the only sounds, except as they brushed against a bench or a table.

Paul of Merely was a brave man, but he shuddered at the thought of dying uselessly at the hands of a mere boy. He would not call upon his friends for aid, but presently, to his relief, Beauchamp sprang between them with drawn sword, crying "Enough, gentlemen, enough! You have no quarrel. Sheathe your swords."

But the boy's only response was, "*En garde, cochon,*" and Beauchamp found himself taking the center of the stage in the place of his friend. Nor did the boy neglect Paul of Merely, but engaged them both in swordplay that caused the eyes of Greystoke to bulge from their sockets.

So swiftly moved his flying blade that half the time it was a sheet of gleaming light, and now he was driving home his thrusts and the smile had frozen upon his lips—grim and stern.

Paul of Merely and Beauchamp were wounded in a dozen places when Greystoke rushed to their aid, and then it was that a little, wiry, gray man leaped agilely from the kitchen doorway, and with drawn sword took his place beside the boy. It was now two against three and the three may have guessed, though they never knew, that they were pitted against the two greatest swordsmen in the world.

"To the death," cried the little gray man, "*à mort, mon fils.*" Scarcely had the words left his lips ere, as though it had but waited permission, the boy's sword flashed into the heart of Paul of Merely, and a Saxon gentleman was gathered to his fathers.

The old man engaged Greystoke now, and the boy turned his undivided attention to Beauchamp. Both these men were considered excellent swordsmen, but when Beauchamp heard again the little gray man's "*à mort, mon fils,*" he shuddered, and the little hairs at the nape of his neck rose up, and his spine froze, for he knew that he had heard the sentence of death passed upon him; for no mortal had yet lived who could vanquish such a swordsman as he who now faced him.

As Beauchamp pitched forward across a bench, dead, the little old man led Greystoke to where the boy awaited him.

"They are thy enemies, my son, and to thee belongs the pleasure of revenge; *à mort, mon fils.*"

Greystoke was determined to sell his life dearly, and he rushed the lad as a great bull might rush a teasing dog, but the boy gave back not an inch and when Greystoke stopped there was a foot of cold steel protruding from his back.

Together they buried the knights at the bottom of the dry moat at the back of the ruined castle. First they had stripped them, and when they took account of the spoils of the combat they found themselves richer by three horses with full trappings, many pieces of gold and silver money, ornaments and jewels, as well as the lances, swords and chain mail armor of their ertswhile guests.

But the greatest gain, the old man thought to himself, was that the knowledge of the remarkable resemblance between his ward and Prince Edward of England had come to him in time to prevent the undoing of his life's work.

The boy, while young, was tall and broad shouldered, and so the old man had little difficulty in fitting one of the suits of armor to him, obliterating the devices so that none might guess to whom it had belonged. This he did, and from then on the boy never rode abroad except in armor, and when he met others upon the high road his visor was always lowered that none might see his face.

The day following the episode of the three knights the old man called the boy to him, saying,

"It is time, my son, that thou learned an answer to such questions as were put to thee yestereve by the pigs of Henry. Thou art fifteen years of age, and thy name be Norman, and so, as this be the ancient castle of Torn, thou mayst answer those whom thou desire to know it that thou art Norman of Torn; that thou be a French gentleman whose father purchased Torn and brought thee hither from France on the death of thy mother, when thou wert six years old.

"But remember, Norman of Torn, that the best answer for an Englishman is the sword; naught else may penetrate his thick wit."

And so was born that Norman of Torn whose name in a few short years was to strike terror to the hearts of Englishmen, and whose power in the vicinity of Torn was greater than that of the King or the barons.

CHAPTER VI

FROM now on the old man devoted himself to the training of the boy in the handling of his lance and battle-axe, but each day also a period was allotted to the sword, until, by the time the youth had turned sixteen, even the old man himself was as but a novice by comparison with the marvelous skill of his pupil.

During these days the boy rode Sir Mortimer abroad in many directions until he knew every bypath within a radius of fifty miles of Torn. Sometimes the old man accompanied him, but more often he rode alone.

On one occasion he chanced upon a hut at the outskirts of a small hamlet not far from Torn, and, with the curiosity of boyhood, determined to enter and have speech with the inmates, for by this time the natural desire for companionship was commencing to assert itself. In all his life he remembered only the company of the old man, who never spoke except when necessity required.

The hut was occupied by an old priest, and as the boy in armor pushed in, without the usual formality of knocking, the old man looked up with an expression of annoyance and disapproval.

"What now," he said, "have the King's men respect neither for piety nor age that they burst in upon the seclusion of a holy man without so much as a 'by your leave'?"

"I am no king's man," replied the boy quietly, "I am

Norman of Torn, who has neither a king nor a god, and who says 'by your leave' to no man. But I have come in peace because I wish to talk to another than my father. Therefore you may talk to me, priest," he concluded with haughty peremptoriness.

"By the nose of John, but it must be a king has deigned to honor me with his commands," laughed the priest. "Raise your visor, My Lord, I would fain look upon the countenance from which issue the commands of royalty."

The priest was a large man with beaming, kindly eyes, and a round jovial face. There was no bite in the tones of his good-natured retort, and so, smiling, the boy raised his visor.

"By the ear of Gabriel," cried the good father, "a child in armor!"

"A child in years, mayhap," replied the boy, "but a good child to own as a friend, if one has enemies who wear swords."

"Then we shall be friends, Norman of Torn, for albeit I have few enemies no man has too many friends, and I like your face and your *manner*, though there be much to wish for in your *manners*. Sit down and eat with me, and I will talk to your heart's content, for be there one other thing I more love than eating, it is talking."

With the priest's aid the boy laid aside his armor, for it was heavy and uncomfortable, and together the two sat down to the meal that was already partially on the board.

Thus began a friendship which lasted during the

lifetime of the good priest. Whenever he could so so Norman of Torn visited his friend, Father Claude. It was he who taught the boy to read and write in French, English and Latin at a time when but few of the nobles could sign their own names.

French was spoken almost exclusively at court and among the higher classes of society, and all public documents were inscribed either in French or Latin, although about this time the first proclamation written in the English tongue was issued by an English king to his subjects.

Father Claude taught the boy to respect the rights of others, to espouse the cause of the poor and weak, to revere God and to believe that the principal reason for man's existence was to protect woman. All of virtue and chivalry and true manhood which his old guardian had neglected to inculcate in the boy's mind the good priest planted there, but he could not eradicate his deep-seated hatred for the English, or his belief that the real test of manhood lay in a desire to fight to the death with a sword.

An occurrence which befell during one of the boy's earlier visits to his new friend rather decided the latter that no arguments he could bring to bear could ever overcome the bald fact that to this very belief of the boy's, and his ability to back it up with acts, the good father owed a great deal, possibly his life.

As they were seated in the priest's hut one afternoon a rough knock fell upon the door which was immediately pushed open to admit as disreputable a band of ruffians as ever polluted the sight of man. Six of them there were, clothed in dirty leather, and wearing swords and daggers at their sides.

The leader was a mighty fellow with a great shock of coarse black hair and a red, bloated face almost concealed by a huge matted black beard. Behind him pushed another giant with red hair and a bristling mustache; while the third was marked by a terrible scar across his left cheek and forehead and from a blow which had evidently put out his left eye, for that socket was empty, and the sunken eyelid but partly covered the inflamed red of the hollow where his eye had been.

"A ha, my hearties," roared the leader, turning to his motley crew, "fine pickings here indeed. A swine of God fattened upon the sweat of such poor honest devils as we, and a young shoat who, by his looks, must have pieces of gold in his belt.

"Say your prayers, my pigeons," he continued, with a vile oath, "for The Black Wolf leaves no evidence behind him to tie his neck with a halter later, and dead men talk the least."

"If it be The Black Wolf," whispered Father Claude to the boy, "no worse fate could befall us for he preys ever upon the clergy, and when drunk as he now is, he murders his victims. I will throw myself before them while you hasten through the rear doorway to your horse, and make good your escape." He spoke in French, and held his hands in the attitude of prayer, so that he quite entirely misled the ruffians, who had no idea that he was communicating with the boy.

Norman of Torn could scarce repress a smile at this

clever ruse of the old priest, and, assuming a similar attitude, he replied in French:

"The good Father Claude does not know Norman of Torn if he thinks he runs out the back door like an old woman because a sword looks in at the front door."

Then rising he addressed the ruffians.

"I do not know what manner of grievance you hold against my good friend here, nor neither do I care. It is sufficient that he is the friend of Norman of Torn, and that Norman of Torn be here in person to acknowledge the debt of friendship. Have at you, sir knights of the great filth and the mighty stink!" and with drawn sword he vaulted over the table and fell upon the surprised leader.

In the little room but two could engage him at once, but so fiercely did his blade swing and so surely did he thrust that in a bare moment The Black Wolf lay dead upon the floor and the red giant, Shandy, was badly though not fatally wounded. The four remaining ruffians backed quickly from the hut, and a more cautious fighter would have let them go their way in peace, for in the open four against one are odds no man may pit himself against with impunity. But Norman of Torn saw red when he fought and the red lured him ever on into the thickest of the fray. Only once before had he fought to the death, but that once had taught him the love of it, and ever after until his death it marked his manner of fighting; so that men who loathed and hated and feared him were as one with those who loved him in acknowledging that never before had God joined in the human frame absolute supremacy with the sword and such utter fearlessness.

So it was, now, that instead of being satisfied with his victory he rushed out after the four knaves. Once in the open, they turned upon him, but he sprang into their midst with his seething blade, and it was as though they faced four men rather than one, so quickly did he parry a thrust here and return a cut there. In a moment one was disarmed, another down, and the remaining two fleeing for their lives toward the high road with Norman of Torn close at their heels.

Young, agile and perfect in health he outclassed them in running as well as in swordsmanship, and ere they had made fifty paces both had thrown away their swords and were on their knees pleading for their lives.

"Come back to the good priest's hut, and we shall see what he may say," replied Norman of Torn.

On the way back they found the man who had been disarmed bending over his wounded comrade. They were brothers, named Flory, and one would not desert the other. It was evident that the wounded man was in no danger, so Norman of Torn ordered the others to assist him into the hut, where they found Red Shandy sitting propped against the wall while the good father poured the contents of a flagon down his eager throat.

The villain's eyes fairly popped from his head when he saw his four comrades coming, unarmed and prisoners, back to the little room.

"The Black Wolf dead, Red Shandy and John Flory wounded, James Flory, One Eye Kanty and Peter the Hermit prisoners!" he ejaculated.

"Man or devil! By the Pope's hind leg, who and what be ye?" he said, turning to Norman of Torn.

"I be your master and ye be my men," said Norman of Torn. "Me ye shall serve in fairer work than ye have selected for yourselves, but with fighting a plenty and good reward."

The sight of this gang of ruffians banded together to prey upon the clergy had given rise to an idea in the boy's mind, which had been revolving in a nebulous way within the innermost recesses of his subconsciousness since his vanquishing of the three knights had brought him, so easily, such riches in the form of horses, arms, armor and gold. As was always his wont in his after life, to think was to act.

"With The Black Wolf dead, and may the devil pull out his eyes with red hot tongs, we might look farther and fare worse, mates, in search of a chief," spoke Red Shandy, eyeing his fellows, "for verily any man, be he but a stripling, who can vanquish six such as we, be fit to command us."

"But what be the duties?" said he whom they called Peter the Hermit.

"To follow Norman of Torn where he may lead, to protect the poor and the weak, to lay down your lives in defence of woman, and to prey upon rich Englishmen and harass the King of England."

The last two clauses of these articles of faith appealed to the ruffians so strongly that they would have subscribed to anything, even daily mass, and a bath, had that been necessary to admit them to the service of Norman of Torn.

"Aye, aye!" they cried. "We be your men indeed."

"Wait," said Norman of Torn, "there is more. You are to obey my every command on pain of instant death, and one-half of all your gains are to be mine. On my side I will clothe and feed you, furnish you with mounts and armor and weapons and a roof to sleep under, and fight for and with you with a sword arm which you know to be no mean protector. Are you satisfied?"

"That we are," and "Long live Norman of Torn," and "Here's to the chief of the Torns" signified the ready assent of the burly cut-throats.

"Then swear it as ye kiss the hilt of my sword and this token," pursued Norman of Torn catching up a crucifix from the priest's table.

With these formalities was born the Clan Torn, which grew in a few years to number a thousand men, and which defied a king's army and helped to make Simon de Montfort virtual ruler of England.

Almost immediately commenced that series of outlaw acts upon neighboring barons, and chance members of the gentry who happened to be caught in the open by the outlaws, that filled the coffers of Norman of Torn with many pieces of gold and silver, and placed a price upon his head ere he had scarce turned eighteen.

That he had no fear of or desire to avoid responsibility for his acts he grimly evidenced by marking with a dagger's point upon the foreheads of those who fell before his own sword the initials NT.

As his following and wealth increased he rebuilt and enlarged the grim Castle of Torn, and again dammed the little stream which had furnished the moat with water in bygone days.

Through all the length and breadth of the country that witnessed his activities his very name was worshipped by poor and lowly and oppressed. The money he took from the King's tax gatherers he returned to the miserable peasants of the district, and once when Henry III sent a little expedition against him he surrounded and captured the entire force, and, stripping them, gave their clothing to the poor, and escorted them naked back to the very gates of London.

By the time he was twenty Norman the Devil, as the King himself had dubbed him, was known by reputation throughout all England, though no man had seen his face and lived, other than his friends and followers. He had become a power to reckon with in the fast culminating quarrel between King Henry and his foreign favorites on one side, and the Saxon and Norman barons on the other.

Neither side knew which way his power might be turned, for Norman of Torn had preyed almost equally upon royalist and insurgent. Personally, he had decided to join neither party, but to take advantage of the turmoil of the times to prey without partiality upon both.

As Norman of Torn approached his grim castle home with his five filthy ragged cut-throats on the day of his first meeting with them, the old man of Torn stood watching the little party from one of the small towers of the barbican.

Halting beneath this outer gate, the youth winded

the horn which hung at his side in mimicry of the custom of the times.

"What ho, without there!" challenged the old man entering grimly into the spirit of the play.

" 'Tis Sir Norman of Torn," spoke up Red Shandy, "with his great host of noble knights and men-at-arms and squires and lackeys and sumpter beasts. Open in the name of the good right arm of Sir Norman of Torn."

"What means this, my son?" said the old man as Norman of Torn dismounted within the ballium.

The youth narrated the events of the morning, concluding with, "These, then, be my men, father; and together we shall fare forth upon the highways and into the byways of England, to collect from the rich English pigs that living which you have ever taught me was owing us."

" 'Tis well, my son, and even as I myself would have it; together we shall ride out, and where we ride a trail of blood shall mark our way.

"From now, henceforth, the name and fame of Norman of Torn shall grow in the land, until even the King shall tremble when he hears it, and shall hate and loathe ye as I have even taught ye to hate and loathe him.

"All England shall curse ye and the blood of Saxon and Norman shall never dry upon your blade."

As the old man walked away toward the great gate of the castle after this outbreak, Shandy, turning to Norman of Torn, with a wide grin, said:

"By the Pope's hind leg, but thy amiable father loveth

the English. There should be great riding after such as he."

"Ye ride after *me*, varlet," cried Norman of Torn, "an' lest ye should forget again so soon who be thy master, take that, as a reminder," and he struck the red giant full upon the mouth with his clenched fist—so that the fellow tumbled heavily to the earth.

He was on his feet in an instant, spitting blood, and in a towering rage. As he rushed, bull-like, toward Norman of Torn, the latter made no move to draw; he but stood with folded arms, eyeing Shandy with cold, level gaze; his head held high, haughty face marked by an arrogant sneer of contempt.

The great ruffian paused, then stopped, slowly a sheepish smile o'erspread his countenance and going upon one knee he took the hand of Norman of Torn and kissed it, as some great and loyal noble knight might have kissed his king's hand in proof of his love and fealty. There was a certain rude, though chivalrous grandeur in the act; and it marked not only the beginning of a lifelong devotion and loyalty on the part of Shandy toward his young master, but was prophetic of the attitude which Norman of Torn was to inspire in all the men who served him during the long years that saw thousands pass the barbicans of Torn to crave a position beneath his grim banner.

As Shandy rose, one by one, John Flory, James, his brother, One Eye Kanty, and Peter the Hermit knelt before their young lord and kissed his hand. From the Great Court beyond a little, grim, gray, old man had watched this scene, a slight smile upon his old, malicious face.

" 'Tis to transcend even my dearest dreams," he muttered. " 'S death, but he be more a king than Henry himself. God speed the day of his coronation, when, before the very eyes of the Plantagenet hound, a black cap shall be placed upon his head for a crown; beneath his feet the platform of a wooden gibbet for a throne."

CHAPTER VII

IT WAS a beautiful spring day in May, 1262, that Norman of Torn rode alone down the narrow trail that led to the pretty cottage with which he had replaced the hut of his old friend Father Claude.

As was his custom he rode with lowered visor, and nowhere upon his person or upon the trappings of his horse were sign or insignia of rank or house. More powerful and richer than many nobles of the court he was without rank or other title than that of outlaw and he scorned to assume what in reality he held in little esteem.

He wore armor because his old guardian had urged him to do so, and not because he craved the protection it afforded. And for the same cause he rode always with lowered visor, though he could never prevail upon the old man to explain the reason which necessitated this precaution.

"It is enough that I tell you, my son," the old fellow was wont to say, "that for your own good as well as mine you must not show your face to your enemies until I so direct. The time will come and soon now, I hope, when you shall uncover your countenance to all England."

The young man gave the matter but little thought, usually passing it off as the foolish whim of an old dotard; but he humored it nevertheless.

Behind him, as he rode down the steep declivity that day, loomed a very different Torn from that which he had approached sixteen years before, when, as a little boy he had ridden through the darkening shadows of the night, perched upon a great horse behind the little old woman, whose metamorphosis to the little grim, gray, old man of Torn their advent to the castle had marked.

Today the great, frowning pile loomed larger and more imposing than ever in the most resplendent days of its past grandeur. The original keep was there with its huge buttressed Saxon towers whose mighty fifteen foot walls were pierced with stairways and vaulted chambers, lighted by embrasures which, mere slits in the outer periphery of the walls, spread to larger dimensions within, some even attaining the area of small triangular chambers.

The moat, widened and deepened, completely encircled three sides of the castle, running between the inner and outer walls, which were set at intervals with small projecting towers so pierced that a flanking fire from long bows, cross bows and javelins might be directed against a scaling party.

The fourth side of the walled enclosure overhung a high precipice, which natural protection rendered towers unnecessary upon this side.

The main gateway of the castle looked toward the west and from it ran the tortuous and rocky trail, down through the mountains toward the valley below. The aspect from the great gate was one of quiet and rugged beauty. A short stretch of barren downs in the foreground only sparsely studded with an occasional gnarled oak gave an unobstructed view of broad and lovely meadow-land through which wound a sparkling tributary of the Trent.

Two more gateways let into the great fortress, one piercing the north wall and one the east. All three gates were strongly fortified with towered and buttressed barbicans which must be taken before the main gates could be reached. Each barbican was portcullised, while the inner gates were similarly safeguarded in addition to the drawbridges which, spanning the moat when lowered, could be drawn up at the approach of an enemy, effectually stopping his advance.

The new towers and buildings added to the ancient keep under the direction of Norman of Torn and the grim, old man whom he called father, were of the Norman type of architecture, the windows were larger, the carving more elaborate, the rooms lighter and more spacious.

Within the great enclosure thrived a fair sized town, for, with his ten hundred fighting-men, the Outlaw of Torn required many squires, lackeys, cooks, scullions, armorers, smithies, farriers, hostlers and the like to care for the wants of his little army.

Fifteen hundred war horses, beside five hundred sumpter beasts, were quartered in the great stables, while the east court was alive with cows, oxen, goats, sheep, pigs, rabbits and chickens.

Great wooden carts drawn by slow, plodding oxen were daily visitors to the grim pile, fetching provender for man and beast from the neighboring farm lands of the poor Saxon peasants to whom Norman of Torn paid good gold for their crops.

These poor serfs, who were worse than slaves to the proud barons who owned the land they tilled, were forbidden by royal edict to sell or give a pennysworth of provisions to the Outlaw of Torn, upon pain of death, but nevertheless his great carts made their trips regularly and always returned full laden, and though the husbandmen told sad tales to their overlords of the awful raids of the Devil of Torn in which he seized upon their stuff by force, their tongues were in their cheeks as they spoke and the Devil's gold in their pockets.

And so, while the barons learned to hate him the more, the peasants' love for him increased. Them he never injured; their fences, their stock, their crops, their wives and daughters were safe from molestation even though the neighboring castle of their lord might be sacked from the wine cellar to the ramparts of the loftiest tower. Nor did anyone dare ride rough shod over the territory which Norman of Torn patrolled. A dozen bands of cut-throats he had driven from the Derby hills, and though the barons would much rather have had all the rest than he, the peasants worshipped him as a deliverer from the lowborn murderers who had been wont to despoil the weak and lowly and on whose account the women of the huts and cottages had never been safe.

Few of them had seen his face and fewer still had spoken with him, but they loved his name and his prowess and in secret they prayed for him to their ancient god Wodin and the lesser gods of the forest and the meadow and the chase, for though they were confessed Christians, still in the hearts of many beat a faint echo of the old superstitions of their ancestors; and while they prayed also to the Lord Jesus and to Mary, yet they felt it could do no harm to be on the safe side with the others, in case they did happen to exist.

A poor, degraded, downtrodden, ignorant, superstitious people, they were; accustomed for generations to the heel of first one invader and then another and in the interims, when there were any, the heels of their feudal lords and their rapacious monarchs.

No wonder then that such as these worshipped the Outlaw of Torn, for since their fierce Saxon ancestors had come, themselves as conquerors, to England no other hand had ever been raised to shield them from oppression.

On this policy of his toward the serfs and freedmen Norman of Torn and the grim, old man whom he called father had never agreed. The latter was for carrying his war of hate against all Englishmen, but the young man would neither listen to it, nor allow any who rode out from Torn to molest the lowly. A ragged tunic was a surer defence against this wild horde than a stout lance or an emblazoned shield.

So, as Norman of Torn rode down from his mighty castle to visit Father Claude, the sunlight playing on his clanking armor and glancing from the copper boss of his shield, the sight of a little group of woodmen kneeling uncovered by the roadside as he passed was not so remarkable after all.

Entering the priest's study, Norman of Torn removed

his armor and lay back moodily upon a bench with his back against a wall and his strong, lithe legs stretched out before him.

"What ails you, my son?" asked the priest, "that you look so disconsolate on this beautiful day?"

"I do not know, Father," replied Norman of Torn, "unless it be that I am asking myself the question, 'What it is all for?' Why did my father train me ever to prey upon my fellows? I like to fight, but there is plenty of fighting which is legitimate, and what good may all my stolen wealth avail me if I may not enter the haunts of men to spend it? Should I stick my head into London town it would doubtless stay there, held by a hempen necklace.

"What quarrel have I with the King or the gentry? They have quarrel enough with me it is true, but, nathless, I do not know why I should have hated them so before I was old enough to know how rotten they really are. So it seems to me that I am but the instrument of an old man's spite, not even knowing the grievance to the avenging of which my life has been dedicated by another.

"And at times, Father Claude, as I grow older, I doubt much that the nameless old man of Torn is my father, so little do I favor him, and never in all my life have I heard a word of fatherly endearment or felt a caress, even as a little child. What think you, Father Claude?"

"I have thought much of it, my son," answered the priest. "It has ever been a sore puzzle to me, and I have my suspicions, which I have held for years, but which even the thought of so frightens me that I shudder to speculate upon the consequences of voicing them aloud. Norman of Torn, if you are not the son of the old man you call father may God forfend that England ever guesses your true parentage. More than this I dare not say except that as you value your peace of mind and your life, keep your visor down and keep out of the clutches of your enemies."

"Then you know why I should keep my visor down?"

"I can only guess, Norman of Torn, because I have seen another whom you resemble."

The conversation was interrupted by a commotion from without; the sound of horses' hoofs, the cries of men and the clash of arms. In an instant both men were at the tiny unglazed window. Before them on the highroad five knights in armor were now engaged in furious battle with a party of ten or a dozen other steel-clad warriors, while crouching breathless on her palfry a young woman sat a little apart from the contestants.

Presently one of the knights detached himself from the mêlée and rode to her side with some word of command, at the same time grasping roughly at her bridle rein. The girl raised her riding whip and struck repeatedly but futilely against the iron headgear of her assailant while he swung his horse up the road, and, dragging her palfrey after him, galloped rapidly out of sight.

Norman of Torn sprang to the door, and, reckless of his unarmored condition, leaped to Sir Mortimer's back and spurred swiftly in the direction taken by the girl and her abductor.

The great black was fleet, and, unencumbered by the

usual heavy armor of his rider, soon brought the fugitives to view. Scarce a mile had been covered ere the knight, turning to look for pursuers, saw the face of Norman of Torn not ten paces behind him.

With a look of mingled surprise, chagrin and incredulity the knight reined in his horse, exclaiming as he did so, "*Mon Dieu*, Edward!"

"Draw and defend yourself," cried Norman of Torn.

"But, Your Highness," stammered the knight.

"Draw, or I stick you as I have stuck an hundred other English pigs," cried Norman of Torn.

The charging steed was almost upon him and the knight looked to see the rider draw rein, but like a black bolt the mighty Sir Mortimer struck the other horse full upon the shoulder, and man and steed rolled in the dust of the roadway.

The knight arose, unhurt, and Norman of Torn dismounted to give fair battle upon even terms. Though handicapped by the weight of his armor the knight also had the advantage of its protection, so that the two fought furiously for several minutes without either gaining an advantage.

The girl sat motionless and wide-eyed at the side of the road watching every move of the two contestants. She made no effort to escape, but seemed riveted to the spot by the very fierceness of the battle she was beholding, as well, possibly, as by the fascination of the handsome giant who had espoused her cause. As she looked upon her champion she saw a lithe, muscular, brown-haired youth whose clear eyes and perfect figure, unconcealed by either bassinet or hauberk, reflected the clean, athletic life of the trained fighting man.

Upon his face hovered a faint, cold smile of haughty pride as the sword arm, displaying its mighty strength and skill in every move, played with the sweating, puffing, steel-clad enemy who hacked and hewed so futilely before him. For all the din of clashing blades and rattling armor, neither of the contestants had inflicted much damage, for the knight could neither force nor insinuate his point beyond the perfect guard of his unarmored foe, who, for his part, found difficulty in penetrating the other's armor.

Finally by dint of his mighty strength, Norman of Torn drove his blade through the meshes of his adversary's mail, and the fellow with a cry of anguish sank limply to the ground.

"Quick, Sir Knight!" cried the girl. "Mount and flee; yonder come his fellows."

And surely, as Norman of Torn turned in the direction from which he had just come, there, racing toward him at full tilt, rode three steel-armored men on their mighty horses.

"Ride, madam," cried Norman of Torn, "for fly I shall not, nor may I, alone, unarmored, and on foot hope more than to momentarily delay these three fellows, but in that time you should easily make your escape—their heavy burdened animals could never o'ertake your fleet palfrey."

As he spoke he took note for the first time of the young woman. That she was a lady of quality was evidenced not alone by the richness of her riding apparel and the trappings of her palfrey, but as well in her noble and haughty demeanor and the proud expression of her beautiful face.

Although at this time nearly twenty years had passed over the head of Norman of Torn he was without knowledge or experience in the ways of women, nor had he ever spoken with a female of quality or position. No woman graced the castle of Torn nor had the boy, within his memory, ever known a mother.

His attitude therefore was much the same toward women as it was toward men, except that he had sworn always to protect them. Possibly in a way he looked up to womankind, if it could be said that Norman of Torn looked up to anything: God, man or devil. It being more his way to look down upon all creatures whom he took the trouble to notice at all.

As his glance rested upon this woman, whom fate had destined to alter the entire course of his life, Norman of Torn saw that she was beautiful, and that she was of that class against whom he had preyed for years with his band of outlaw cut-throats. Then he turned once more to face her enemies with the strange inconsistency which had ever marked his methods.

Tomorrow he might be assaulting the ramparts of her father's castle, but today he was joyously offering to sacrifice his life for her—had she been the daughter of a charcoal burner he would have done no less—it was enough that she was a woman and in need of protection.

The three knights were now fairly upon him, and with fine disregard for fair play charged with couched spears the unarmored man on foot. But as the leading knight came close enough to behold his face, he cried out in surprise and consternation:

"*Mon Dieu, le Prince!*" He wheeled his charging horse to one side. His fellows, hearing his cry, followed his example, and the three of them dashed on down the high road in as evident anxiety to escape as they had been keen to attack.

"One would think they had met the devil," muttered Norman of Torn, looking after them in unfeigned astonishment.

"What means it, lady?" he asked turning to the damsel, who had made no move to escape.

"It means that your face is well known in your father's realm, my Lord Prince," she replied. "And the King's men have no desire to antagonize you even though they may understand as little as I why you should espouse the cause of a daughter of Simon de Montfort."

"Am I then taken for Prince Edward of England?" he asked.

"An' who else should you be taken for, my Lord?"

"I am not the Prince," said Norman of Torn. "It is said that Edward is in France."

"Right you are, sir," exclaimed the girl. "I had not thought on that; but you be enough of his likeness that you might well deceive the Queen herself. And you be of a bravery fit for a king's son. Who are you then, Sir Knight, who has bared your steel and faced death for Bertrade, daughter of Simon de Montfort, Earl of Leicester?"

"Be you De Montfort's daughter, niece of King

Henry?" queried Norman of Torn, his eyes narrowing to mere slits and face hardening.

"That I be," replied the girl, "an' from your face I take it you have little love for a De Montfort," she added, smiling.

"An' whither may you be bound, Lady Bertrade de Montfort? Be you niece or daughter of the devil, yet still you be a woman, and I do not war against women. Wheresoever you would go will I accompany you to safety."

"I was but now bound, under escort of five of my father's knights, to visit Mary, daughter of John de Stutevill of Derby."

"I know the castle well," answered Norman of Torn, and the shadow of a grim smile played about his lips, for scarce sixty days had elapsed since he had reduced the stronghold, and levied tribute on the great baron. "Come, you have not far to travel now, and if we make haste you shall sup with your friend before dark."

So saying, he mounted his horse and was turning to retrace their steps down the road when he noticed the body of the dead knight lying where it had fallen.

"Ride on," he called to Bertrade de Montfort, "I will join you in an instant."

Again dismounting he returned to the side of his late adversary, and lifting the dead knight's visor drew upon the forehead with the point of his dagger the letters NT.

The girl turned to see what detained him, but his back was toward her and he knelt beside his fallen foeman, and she did not see his act. Brave daughter of a brave sire though she was, had she seen what he did her heart would have quailed within her and she would have fled in terror from the clutches of this scourge of England, whose mark she had seen on the dead foreheads of a dozen of her father's knights and kinsmen.

Their way to Stutevill lay past the cottage of Father Claude, and here Norman of Torn stopped to don his armor. Now he rode once more with lowered visor, and in silence, a little to the rear of Bertrade de Montfort that he might watch her face, which, of a sudden, had excited his interest.

Never before, within the scope of his memory, had he been so close to a young and beautiful woman for so long a period of time, although he had often seen women in the castles that had fallen before his vicious and terrible attacks. While stories were abroad of his vile treatment of women captives, there was no truth in them. They were merely spread by his enemies to incite the people against him. Never had Norman of Torn laid violent hand upon a woman, and his cutthroat band were under oath to respect and protect the sex, on penalty of death.

As he watched the semi-profile of the lovely face before him, something stirred in his heart which had been struggling for expression for years. It was not love, nor was it allied to love, but a deep longing for companionship of such as she, and such as she represented. Norman of Torn could not have translated this feeling into words for he did not know, but it was the far faint cry of blood for blood and with it, mayhap, was mixed not alone the longing of the lion among jackals for other lions, but for his lioness.

They rode for many miles in silence when suddenly she turned, saying:

"You take your time, Sir Knight, in answering my query. Who be ye?"

"I am Nor—" and then he stopped. Always before he had answered that question with haughty pride. Why should he hesitate, he thought. Was it because he feared the loathing that name would inspire in the breast of this daughter of the aristocracy he despised? Did Norman of Torn fear to face the look of scorn and repugnance that was sure to be mirrored in that lovely face?

"I am from Normandy," he went on quietly. "A gentleman of France."

"But your name?" she said peremptorily. "Are you ashamed of your name?"

"You may call me Roger," he answered. "Roger de Condé."

"Raise your visor, Roger de Condé," she commanded. "I do not take pleasure in riding with a suit of armor; I would see that there is a man within."

Norman of Torn smiled as he did her bidding, and when he smiled thus, as he rarely did, he was good to look upon.

"It is the first command I have obeyed since I turned sixteen, Bertrade de Montfort," he said.

The girl was about nineteen, full of the vigor and gaiety of youth and health; and so the two rode on their journey talking and laughing as they might have been friends of long standing.

She told him of the reason for the attack upon her

earlier in the day, attributing it to an attempt on the part of a certain baron, Peter of Colfax, to abduct her, his suit for her hand having been peremptorily and roughly denied by her father.

Simon de Montfort was no man to mince words, and it is doubtless that the old reprobate who sued for his daughter's hand heard some unsavory truths from the man who had twice scandalized England's nobility by his rude and discourteous, though true and candid, speeches to the King.

"This Peter of Colfax shall be looked to," growled Norman of Torn. "And as you have refused his heart and hand, his head shall be yours for the asking. You have but to command, Bertrade de Montfort."

"Very well," she laughed, thinking it but the idle boasting so much indulged in in those days. "You may bring me his head upon a golden dish, Roger de Condé."

"And what reward does the knight earn who brings to the feet of his princess the head of her enemy?" he asked lightly.

"What boon would the knight ask?"

"That whatsoever a bad report you hear of your knight, of whatsoever calumnies may be heaped upon him, you shall yet ever be his friend, and believe in his honor and his loyalty."

The girl laughed gaily as she answered, though something seemed to tell her that this was more than play.

"It shall be as you say, Sir Knight," she replied. "And the boon once granted shall be always kept."

Quick to reach decisions and as quick to act, Norman

of Torn decided that he liked this girl and that he wished her friendship more than any other thing he knew of. And wishing it, he determined to win it by any means that accorded with his standard of honor; an honor which in many respects was higher than that of the nobles of his time.

They reached the castle of De Stutevill late in the afternoon, and there Norman of Torn was graciously welcomed and urged to accept the Baron's hospitality over night.

The grim humor of the situation was too much for the outlaw, and, when added to his new desire to be in the company of Bertrade de Montfort, he made no effort to resist, but hastened to accept the warm welcome.

At the long table upon which the evening meal was spread sat the entire household of the Baron, and here and there among the men were evidences of painful wounds but barely healed, while the host himself still wore his sword arm in a sling.

"We have been through grievous times," said Sir John, noticing that his guest was glancing at the various evidences of conflict. "That fiend, Norman the Devil, with his filthy pack of cut-throats besieged us for ten days, and then took the castle by storm and sacked it. Life is no longer safe in England with the King spending his time and money with foreign favorites and buying alien soldiery to fight against his own barons, instead of insuring the peace and protection which is the right of every Englishman at home.

"But," he continued, "this outlaw devil will come to

the end of a short halter when once our civil strife is settled, for the barons themselves have decided upon an expedition against him, if the King will not subdue him."

"An' he may send the barons naked home as he did the King's soldiers," laughed Bertrade de Montfort. "I should like to see this fellow; what may he look like—from the appearance of yourself, Sir John, and many of your men-at-arms there should be no few here but have met him."

"Not once did he raise his visor while he was among us," replied the Baron, "but there are those who claim they had a brief glimpse of him and that he is of horrid countenance, wearing a great yellow beard and having one eye gone, and a mighty red scar from his forehead to his chin."

"A fearful apparition," murmured Norman of Torn. "No wonder he keeps his helm closed."

"But such a swordsman," spoke up a son of De Stutevill. "Never in all the world was there such sword play as I saw that day in the courtyard."

"I, too, have seen some wonderful sword play," said Bertrade de Montfort, "and that today. O ho!" she cried, laughing gleefully, "verily do I believe I have captured the wild Norman of Torn, for this very knight, who styles himself Roger de Condé, fights as I ne'er saw man fight before, and he rode with his visor down until I chid him for it."

Norman of Torn led in the laugh which followed, and of all the company he most enjoyed the joke.

"An' speaking of the Devil," said the Baron, "how

think you he will side should the King eventually force war upon the barons? With his thousand hell-hounds the fate of England might well lie in the palm of his bloody hand."

"He loves neither King nor baron," spoke Mary de Stutevill, "and I rather lean to the thought that he will serve neither, but rather plunder the castles of both rebel and royalist whilst their masters be absent at war."

"It be more to his liking to come while the master be home to welcome him," said De Stutevill, ruthfully. "But yet I am always in fear for the safety of my wife and daughters when I be away from Derby for any time. May the good God soon deliver England from this Devil of Torn."

"I think you may have no need of fear on that score," spoke Mary, "for Norman of Torn offered no violence to any woman within the wall of Stutevill, and when one of his men laid a heavy hand upon me, it was the great outlaw himself who struck the fellow such a blow with his mailed hand as to crack the ruffian's helm, saying at the time, 'Know you, fellow, Norman of Torn does not war upon women?'"

Presently the conversation turned to other subjects and Norman of Torn heard no more of himself during that evening.

His stay at the castle of Stutevill was drawn out to three days, and then, on the third day, as he sat with Bertrade de Montfort in an embrasure of the south tower of the old castle, he spoke once more of the necessity for leaving and once more she urged him to remain.

"To be with you, Bertrade of Montfort," he said boldly, "I would forego any other pleasure, and endure any privation, or face any danger, but there are others who look to me for guidance and my duty calls me away from you. You shall see me again, and at the castle of your father, Simon de Montfort, in Leicester. Provided," he added, "that you will welcome me there."

"I shall always welcome you, wherever I may be, Roger de Condé," replied the girl.

"Remember that promise," he said smiling. "Some day you may be glad to repudiate it."

"Never," she insisted, and a light that shone in her eyes as she said it would have meant much to a man better versed in the ways of women than was Norman of Torn.

"I hope not," he said gravely. "I cannot tell you, being but poorly trained in courtly ways, what I should like to tell you, that you might know how much your friendship means to me. Goodbye, Bertrade de Montfort," and he bent to one knee, as he raised her fingers to his lips.

As he passed over the drawbridge and down toward the highroad a few minutes later on his way back to Torn, he turned for one last look at the castle and there in an embrasure in the south tower stood a young woman who raised her hand to wave, and then, as though by sudden impulse, threw a kiss after the departing knight, only to disappear from the embrasure with the act.

As Norman of Torn rode back to his grim castle in the hills of Derby he had much food for thought upon the way. Never till now had he realized what might lie in another manner of life, and he felt a twinge of bitterness toward the hard old man whom he called father, and whose teachings from the boy's earliest childhood had guided him in the ways that had cut him off completely from the society of other men, except the wild horde of outlaws, ruffians and adventurers that rode beneath the grisly banner of the young chief of Torn.

Only in an ill-defined, nebulous way did he feel that it was the girl who had come into his life that caused him for the first time to feel shame for his past deeds. He did not know the meaning of love, and so he could not know that he loved Bertrade de Montfort.

And another thought which now filled his mind was the fact of his strange likeness to the Crown Prince of England. This, together with the words of Father Claude, puzzled him sorely. What might it mean? Was it a heinous offence to own an accidental likeness to a king's son?

But now that he felt he had solved the reason that he rode always with closed helm he was for the first time anxious himself to hide his face from the sight of men. Not from fear, for he knew not fear, but from some inward impulse which he did not attempt to fathom.

CHAPTER VIII

AS Norman of Torn rode out from the castle of De
Stutevill, Father Claude dismounted from his sleek
donkey within the ballium of Torn. The austere stronghold, notwithstanding its repellent exterior and unsavory reputation, always extended a warm welcome to
the kindly, genial priest; not alone because of the deep
friendship which the master of Torn felt for the good
father, but through the personal charm, and lovable-
ness of the holy man's nature, which shone alike on
saint and sinner.

It was doubtless due to his unremitting labors with
the youthful Norman, during the period that the boy's
character was most amenable to strong impressions,
that the policy of the mighty outlaw was in many respects pure and lofty. It was this same influence,
though, which won for Father Claude his only enemy
in Torn; the little, grim, gray, old man whose sole aim
in life seemed to have been to smother every finer
instinct of chivalry and manhood in the boy, to whose
training he had devoted the past nineteen years of
his life.

As Father Claude climbed down from his donkey—
fat people do not "dismount"—a half dozen young
squires ran forward to assist him, and to lead the animal
to the stables.

The good priest called each of his willing helpers
by name, asking a question here, passing a merry joke

there with the ease and familiarity that bespoke mutual affection and old acquaintance.

As he passed in through the great gate the men-at-arms threw him laughing, though respectful, welcomes and within the great court, beautified with smooth lawn, beds of gorgeous plants, fountains, statues and small shrubs and bushes, he came upon the giant, Red Shandy, now the principal lieutenant of Norman of Torn.

"Good morrow, Saint Claude!" cried the burly ruffian. "Hast come to save our souls, or damn us? What manner of sacrilege have we committed now, or have we merited the blessings of Holy Church? Dost come to scold, or praise?"

"Neither, thou unregenerate villain," cried the priest, laughing. "Though methinks ye merit chiding for the grievous poor courtesy with which thou didst treat the great Bishop of Norwich the past week."

"Tut, tut, Father," replied Red Shandy. "We did but aid him to adhere more closely to the injunctions and precepts of Him whose servant and disciple he claims to be. Were it not better for an Archbishop of His Church to walk in humility and poverty among His people, than to be ever surrounded with the temptations of fine clothing, jewels and much gold, to say nothing of two sumpter beats heavy laden with runlets of wine?"

"I warrant his temptations were less by at least as many runlets of wine as may be borne by two sumpter beasts when thou, red robber, had finished with him," exclaimed Father Claude.

"Yes, Father," laughed the great fellow, "for the sake of Holy Church I did indeed confiscate that temptation completely, and if you must needs have proof in order to absolve me from my sins, come with me now and you shall sample the excellent discrimination which the Bishop of Norwich displays in the selection of his temptations."

"They tell me you left the great man quite destitute of finery, Red Shandy," continued Father Claude, as he locked his arm in that of the outlaw and proceeded toward the castle.

"One garment was all that Norman of Torn would permit him, and as the sun was hot overhead he selected for the Bishop a bassinet for that single article of apparel, to protect his tonsured pate from the rays of old sol. Then fearing that it might be stolen from him by some vandals of the road he had One Eye Kanty rivet it at each side of the gorget so that it could not be removed by other than a smithy, and thus, strapped face to tail upon a donkey, he sent the great Bishop of Norwich rattling down the dusty road with his head, at least, protected from the idle gaze of whomsoever he might chance to meet. Forty stripes he gave to each of the Bishop's retinue for being abroad in bad company; but come, here we are where you shall have the wine as proof of my tale."

As the two sat sipping the Bishop's good Canary the little old man of Torn entered. He spoke to Father Claude in a surly tone, asking him if he knew aught of the whereabouts of Norman of Torn.

"We have seen nothing of him since, some three

days gone, he rode out in the direction of your cottage," he concluded.

"Why, yes," said the priest, "I saw him that day. He had an adventure with several knights from the castle of Peter of Colfax, from whom he rescued a damsel whom I suspect from the trappings of her palfrey to be of the house of Montfort. Together they rode north, but thy son did not say whither or for what purpose. His only remark, as he donned his armor, while the girl waited without, was that I should now behold the falcon guarding the dove. Hast he not returned?"

"No," said the old man, "and doubtless his adventure is of a nature in line with thy puerile and effeminate teachings. Had he followed my training, without thy accurst priestly interference, he had made an iron-barred nest in Torn for many of the doves of thy damned English nobility. An' thou leave him not alone he will soon be seeking service in the household of the King."

"Where, perchance, he might be more at home than here," said the priest quietly.

"Why say you that?" snapped the little old man, eyeing Father Claude narrowly.

"Oh," laughed the priest, "because he whose power and mien be even more kingly than the King's would rightly grace the royal palace," but he had not failed to note the perturbation his remark had caused, nor did his off-hand reply entirely deceive the old man.

At this juncture a squire entered to say that Shandy's presence was required at the gates, and that worthy, with a sorrowing and regretful glance at the unemptied flagon, left the room.

For a few moments the two men sat in meditative silence, which was presntly broken by the old man of Torn.

"Priest," he said, "thy ways with my son are, as you know, not to my liking. It were needless that he should have wasted so much precious time from sword play to learn the useless art of letters. Of what benefit may a knowledge of Latin be to one whose doom looms large before him. It may be years and again it may be but months, but as sure as there be a devil in hell, Norman of Torn will swing from a king's gibbet. And thou knowst it, and he too, as well as I. The things which thou hast taught him be above his station, and the hopes and ambitions they inspire will but make his end the bitterer for him. Of late I have noted that he rides upon the highway with less enthusiasm than was his wont, but he has gone too far ever to go back now; nor is there where to go back to. What has he ever been other than outcast and outlaw? What hopes could you have engendered in his breast greater than to be hated and feared among his blood enemies?"

"I knowst not thy reasons, old man," replied the priest, "for devoting thy life to the ruining of his, and what I guess at be such as I dare not voice; but let us understand each other once and for all. For all thou dost and hast done to blight and curse the nobleness of his nature, I have done and shall continue to do all in my power to controvert. As thou hast been his bad angel, so shall I try to be his good angel, and when all is said and done and Norman of Torn swings from the King's gibbet, as I only too well fear he must, there will be more to mourn his loss than there be to curse him.

"His friends are from the ranks of the lowly, but so too were the friends and followers of our Dear Lord Jesus; so that shall be more greatly to his honor than had he preyed upon the already unfortunate.

"Women have never been his prey; that also will be spoken of to his honor when he is gone, and that he has been cruel to men will be forgotten in the greater glory of his mercy to the weak.

"Whatever be thy object: whether revenge or the natural bent of a cruel and degraded mind, I know not; but if any be curst because of the Outlaw of Torn it will be thou—I had almost said, unnatural father; but I do not believe a single drop of thy debased blood flows in the veins of him thou callest son."

The grim old man of Torn had sat motionless throughout this indictment, his face, somewhat pale, was drawn into lines of malevolent hatred and rage, but he permitted Father Claude to finish without interruption.

"Thou hast made thyself and thy opinions quite clear," he said bitterly, "but I be glad to know just how thou standeth. In the past there has been peace between us, though no love; now let us both understand that it be war and hate. My life work is cut out for me. Others, like thyself, have stood in my path, yet today I am here, but where are they? Dost understand me, priest?" And the old man leaned far across the table so that his eyes, burning with an insane fire of venom, blazed but a few inches from those of the priest.

Father Claude returned the look with calm level gaze.

"I understand," he said, and, rising, left the castle.

Shortly after he had reached his cottage a loud knock sounded at the door, which immediately swung open without waiting the formality of permission. Father Claude looked up to see the tall figure of Norman of Torn, and his face lighted with a pleased smile of welcome.

"Greetings, my son," said the priest.

"And to thee, Father," replied the outlaw, "And what may be the news of Torn, I have been absent for several days; is all well at the castle?"

"All be well at the castle," replied Father Claude, "if by that you mean have none been captured or hanged for their murders. Ah, my boy, why wilt thou not give up this wicked life of thine? It has never been my way to scold or chide thee, yet always hath my heart ached for each crime laid at the door of Norman of Torn."

"Come, come, Father," replied the outlaw, "what dost I that I have not good example for from the barons, and the King, and Holy Church. Murder, theft, rapine! Passeth a day over England which sees not one or all perpetrated in the name of some of these?

"Be it wicked for Norman of Torn to prey upon the wolf, yet righteous for the wolf to tear the sheep? Methinks not. Only do I collect from those who have more than they need, from my natural enemies; while they prey upon those who have naught.

"Yet," and his manner suddenly changed, "I do not

95

love it, Father. That thou know. I would that there might be some way out of it, but there is none.

"If I told you why I wished it you would be surprised indeed, nor can I myself understand; but, of a verity, my greatest wish to be out of this life is due to the fact that I crave the association of those very enemies I have been taught to hate. But it is too late, Father, there can be but one end and that the lower end of a hempen rope."

"No, my son, there is another way, an honorable way," replied the good Father. "In some foreign clime there be opportunities abundant for such as thee. France offers a magnificent future to such a soldier as Norman of Torn. In the court of Louis you would take your place among the highest of the land. You be rich and brave and handsome, nay do not raise your hand, you be all these and more, for you have learning far beyond the majority of nobles, and you have a good heart and a true chivalry of character. With such wondrous gifts naught could bar your way to the highest pinnacles of power and glory, while here you have no future beyond the halter. Canst thou hesitate, Norman of Torn?"

The young man stood silent for a moment, then he drew his hand across his eyes as though to brush away a vision.

"There be a reason, Father, why I must remain in England for a time at least, though the picture you put is indeed wondrous alluring."

And the reason was Bertrade de Montfort.

CHAPTER IX

THE visit of Bertrade de Montfort with her friend Mary de Stutevill was drawing to a close. Three weeks had passed since Roger de Condé had ridden out from the portals of Stutevill and many times the handsome young knight's name had been on the lips of his fair hostess and her fairer friend.

Today the two girls roamed slowly through the gardens of the great court, their arms about each other's waists, pouring the last confidences into each other's ears, for tomorrow Bertrade had elected to return to Leicester.

"Methinks thou be very rash indeed, my Bertrade," said Mary. "Wert my father here he would, I am sure, not permit thee to leave with only the small escort which we be able to give."

"Fear not, Mary," replied Bertrade, "five of thy father's knights be ample protection for so short a journey. By evening it will have been accomplished; and as the only one I fear in these parts received such a sound set back from Roger de Condé recently I do not think he will venture again to molest me."

"But what about the Devil of Torn, Bertrade?" urged Mary. "Only yestereve, you wot, one of Lord de Grey's men-at-arms came limping to us with the news of the awful carnage the foul fiend had wrought on his master's household. He be abroad, Bertrade, and I canst think of naught more horrible than to fall into his hands."

"Why, Mary, thou didst but recently say thy very self that Norman of Torn was most courteous to thee when he sacked this, thy father's castle. How be it thou so soon has changed thy mind?"

"Yes, Bertrade, he was indeed respectful then, but who knows what horrid freak his mind may take, and they do say that he be cruel beyond compare. Again, forget not that thou be Leicester's daughter and Henry's niece; against both of whom the Outlaw of Torn openly swears his hatred and his vengeance. Oh, Bertrade, wait but for a day or so, I be sure my father must return ere then, and fifty knights shall accompany thee instead of five."

"What be fifty knights against Norman of Torn, Mary? Thy reasoning is on a parity with thy fears, both have flown wide of the mark.

"If I am to meet with this wild ruffian it were better that five knights were sacrificed than fifty, for either number would be but a mouthful to that horrid horde of unhung murderers. No, Mary, I shall start tomorrow and your good knights shall return the following day with the best of word from me."

"If thou wilst, thou wilst," cried Mary petulantly. "Indeed it were plain that thou be a De Montfort; that race whose historic bravery be second only to their historic stubbornness."

Bertrade de Montfort laughed, and kissed her friend upon the cheek.

"Mayhap I shall find the brave Roger de Condé again upon the highroad to protect me. Then indeed shall I send back your five knights, for of a truth his blade is more powerful than that of any ten men I ere saw fight before."

"Methinks," said Mary, still peeved at her friend's determination to leave on the morrow, "that should you meet the doughty Sir Roger all unarmed that still would you send back my father's knights."

Bertrade flushed, and then bit her lip as she felt the warm blood mount to her cheek.

"Thou be a fool, Mary," she said.

Mary broke into a joyful, teasing laugh; hugely enjoying the discomfiture of the admission the tell-tale flush proclaimed.

"Ah, I did but guess how thy heart and thy mind tended, Bertrade; but now I seest that I divined all too truly. He be indeed good to look upon, but what knowest thou of him?"

"Hush, Mary!" commanded Bertrade. "Thou know not what thou sayest. I would not wipe my feet upon him, I care naught whatever for him, and then—it has been three weeks since he rode out from Stutevill and no word hath he sent."

"Oh, ho," cried the little plague, "so there lies the wind? My Lady would not wipe her feet upon him, but she be sore vexed that he has sent her no word. *Mon Dieu*, but thou hast strange notions, Bertrade."

"I will not talk with you, Mary," cried Bertrade, stamping her sandaled foot, and with a toss of her pretty head she turned abruptly toward the castle.

In a small chamber in the castle of Colfax two men sat at opposite sides of a little table. The one, Peter of Colfax, was short and very stout. His red, bloated face, bleary eyes and bulbous nose bespoke the manner of his life; while his thick lips, the lower hanging large and flabby over his receding chin, indicated the base passions to which his life and been given. His companion was a little, grim, gray man but his suit of armor and closed helm gave no hint to his host of whom his guest might be. It was the little armored man who was speaking.

"Is it not enough that I offer to aid you, Sir Peter," he said, "that you must have my reasons? Let it go that my hate of Leicester be the passion which moves me. Thou failed in thy attempt to capture the maiden; give me ten knights and I will bring her to you."

"How knowest thou she rides out tomorrow for her father's castle?" asked Peter of Colfax.

"That again be no concern of thine, my friend, but I do know it, and, if thou wouldst have her, be quick, for we should ride out tonight that we may take our positions by the highway in ample time tomorrow."

Still Peter of Colfax hesitated, he feared this might be a ruse of Leicester's to catch him in some trap. He did not know his guest—the fellow might want the girl for himself and be taking this method of obtaining the necessary assistance to capture her.

"Come," said the little, armored man irritably. "I cannot bide here forever. Make up thy mind; it be nothing to me other than my revenge, and if thou wilst not do it I shall hire the necessary ruffians and then not even thou shalt see Bertrade de Montfort more."

This last threat decided the Baron.

"It is agreed," he said. "The men shall ride out with you in half an hour. Wait below, in the courtyard."

When the little man had left the apartment Peter of Colfax summoned his squire whom he had send to him at once one of his faithful henchmen.

"Guy," said Peter of Colfax, as the man entered, "ye made a rare fizzle of a piece of business some weeks ago. Ye wot of which I speak?"

"Yes, My Lord."

"It chances that on the morrow ye may have opportunity to retrieve thy blunder. Ride out with ten men where the stranger who waits in the courtyard below shall lead ye, and come not back without that which ye lost to a handful of men before. You understand?"

"Yes, My Lord!"

"And, Guy, I half mistrust this fellow who hath offered to assist us. At the first sign of treachery fall upon him with all thy men and slay him. Tell the others that these be my orders."

"Yes, My Lord. When do we ride?"

"At once. You may go."

The morning that Bertrade de Montfort had chosen to return to her father's castle dawned gray and threatening. In vain did Mary de Stutevill plead with her friend to give up the idea of setting out upon such a dismal day and without sufficient escort, but Bertrade de Montfort was firm.

"Already have I overstayed my time three days, and it is not lightly that even I, his daughter, fail in obedience to Simon de Montfort. I shall have enough to account for as it be. Do not urge me to add even one more day to my excuses. And again, perchance, my mother and my father may be sore distressed by my continued absence. No, Mary, I must ride today." And so she did, with the five knights that could be spared from the castle's defence.

Scarcely half an hour had elapsed before a cold drizzle set in, so that they were indeed a sorry company that splashed along the muddy road, wrapped in mantle and surcoat. As they proceeded the rain and wind increased in volume, until it was being driven into their faces in such blinding gusts that they must needs keep their eyes closed and trust to the instincts of their mounts.

Less than half the journey had been accomplished. They were winding across a little hollow toward a low ridge covered with dense forest, into the somber shadows of which the road wound. There was a glint of armor among the drenched foliage, but the rain-buffeted eyes of the riders saw it not. On they came, their patient horses plodding slowly through the sticky road and hurtling storm.

Now they were half way up the ridge's side. There was a movement in the dark shadows of the grim wood, and then without cry or warning a band of steel-clad horsemen broke forth with couched spears. Charging at full run down upon them they overthrew three of the girl's escort before a blow could be struck in her defense. Her two remaining guardians wheeled to meet the return attack, and nobly did they acquit themselves, for it took the entire eleven who were pitted against them to overcome and slay the two.

In the mêleé none had noticed the girl, but presently one of her assailants, a little, grim, gray man, discovered that she had put spurs to her palfrey and escaped. Calling to his companions he set out at a rapid pace in pursuit.

Reckless of the slippery road and the blinding rain, Bertrade de Montfort urged her mount into a wild run, for she had recognized the arms of Peter of Colfax on the shields of several of the attacking party.

Nobly the beautiful Arab bent to her call for speed. The great beasts of her pursuers, bred in Normandy and Flanders, might have been tethered in their stalls for all the chance they had of overtaking the flying white steed that fairly split the gray rain as lightning flies through the clouds.

But for the fiendish cunning of the little grim, gray man's foresight Bertrade de Montfort would have made good her escape that day. As it was, however, her fleet mount had carried her but two hundred yards ere, in the midst of the dark wood, she ran full upon a rope stretched across the roadway, between two trees.

As the horse fell, with a terrible lunge, tripped by the stout rope, Bertrade de Montfort was thrown far before him, where she lay, a little, limp bedraggled figure, in the mud of the road.

There they found her. The little, grim, gray man did not even dismount, so indifferent was he to her fate; dead or in the hands of Peter of Colfax, it was all the same to him. In either event his purpose would be accomplished, and Bertrade de Montfort would no longer lure Norman of Torn from the path he had laid out for him.

That such an eventuality threatened he knew from one Spizo the Spaniard, the single traitor in the service of Norman of Torn, whose mean aid the little grim, gray man had purchased since many months to spy upon the comings and goings of the great outlaw.

The men of Peter of Colfax gathered up the lifeless form of Bertrade de Montfort and placed it across the saddle before one of their number.

"Come," said the man called Guy, "if there be life left in her we must hasten to Sir Peter before it be extinct."

"I leave ye here," said the little old man. "My part of the business is done."

And so he sat watching them until they had disappeared in the forest toward the castle of Colfax.

Then he rode back to the scene of the encounter where lay the five knights of Sir John de Stutevill. Three were already dead, the other two, sorely but not mortally wounded, lay groaning by the roadside.

The little grim, gray man dismounted as he came abreast of them and with his long sword silently finished the two wounded men. Then, drawing his dagger, he made a mark upon the dead foreheads of each of the five, and mounting, rode rapidly toward Torn.

"And if one fact be not enough," he muttered, "that mark upon the dead will quite effectually stop further intercourse between the houses of Torn and Leicester."

Henry de Montfort, son of Simon, rode fast and furious at the head of a dozen of his father's knights on the road to Stutevill.

Bertrade de Montfort was so long overdue that the Earl and Princess Eleanor, his wife, filled with grave apprehensions, had posted their oldest son off to the castle of John de Stutevill to fetch her home.

With the wind and rain at their backs the little party rode rapidly along the muddy road, until late in the afternoon they came upon a white palfrey standing huddled beneath a great oak, his arched back toward the driving storm.

"By God," cried De Montfort, " 'tis my sister's own Abdul. There be something wrong here indeed." But a rapid search of the vicinity, and loud calls brought no further evidence of the girl's whereabouts, so they pressed on toward Stutevill.

Some two miles beyond the spot where the white palfrey had been found they came upon the dead bodies of the five knights who had accompanied Bertrade from Stutevill.

Dismounting, Henry de Montfort examined the bodies of the fallen men. The arms upon shield and helm confirmed his first fear that these had been Bertrade's escort from Stutevill.

As he bent over them to see if he recognized any of the knights there stared up into his face from the foreheads of the dead men the dreaded sign, NT, scratched there with a dagger's point.

"The curse of God be on him!" cried De Montfort. "It be the work of the Devil of Torn, my gentlemen," he said to his followers. "Come, we need no further guide to our destination." And, remounting, the little party spurred back toward Torn.

When Bertrade de Montfort regained her senses she was in bed in a strange room, and above her bent an old woman; a repulsive, toothless old woman, whose smile was but a fangless snarl.

"Ho, ho!" she croaked. "The bride waketh. I told My Lord that it would take more than a tumble in the mud to kill a De Montfort. Come, come, now, arise and clothe thyself, for the handsome bridegroom canst scarce restrain his eager desire to fold thee in his arms. Below in the great hall he paces to and fro, the red blood mantling his beauteous countenance."

"Who be ye?" cried Bertrade de Montfort, her mind still dazed from the effects of her fall. "Where am I?" and then, "O, *Mon Dieu!*" as she remembered the events of the afternoon; and the arms of Colfax upon the shields of the attacking party. In an instant she realized the horror of her predicament; its utter hopelessness.

Beast though he was, Peter of Colfax stood high in the favor of the King; and the fact that she was his niece would scarce aid her cause with Henry, for it was more than counter-balanced by the fact that she was the daughter of Simon de Montfort, whom he feared and hated.

In the corridor without she heard the heavy tramp of approaching feet, and presently a man's voice at the door.

"Within there, Coll! Hast the damsel awakened from her swoon?"

"Yes, Sir Peter," replied the old woman, "I was but just urging her to arise and clothe herself, saying that you awaited her below."

"Haste then, My Lady Bertrade," called the man, "no harm will be done thee if thou showest the good sense I give thee credit for. I will await thee in the great hall, or, if thou prefer, wilt come to thee here."

The girl paled, more in loathing and contempt than in fear, but the tones of her answer were calm and level.

"I will see thee below, Sir Peter, anon," and rising, she hastened to dress, while the receding footsteps of the Baron diminished down the stairway which led from the tower room in which she was imprisoned.

The old woman attempted to draw her into conversation, but the girl would not talk. Her whole mind was devoted to weighing each possible means of escape.

A half hour later she entered the great hall of the castle of Peter of Colfax. The room was empty. Little change had been wrought in the apartment since the days of Ethelwolf. As the girl's glance ranged the hall in search of her jailer it rested upon the narrow, unglazed windows beyond which lay freedom. Would she ever again breathe God's pure air outside these stifling walls? These grimy hateful walls! Black as the inky rafters and wainscot except for occasional splotches a few shades less begrimed, where repairs had been made. As her eyes fell upon the trophies of war and chase which hung there her lips curled in scorn, for she knew that they were acquisitions by inheritance rather than by the personal prowess of the present master of Colfax.

A single cresset lighted the chamber, while the flickering light from a small wood fire upon one of the two great hearths seemed rather to accentuate the dim shadows of the place.

Bertrade crossed the room and leaned against a massive oak table, blackened by age and hard usage to the color of the beams above, dented and nicked by the pounding of huge drinking horns and heavy swords when wild and lusty brawlers had been moved to applause by the lay of some wandering minstrel, or the sterner call of their mighty chieftains for the oath of fealty.

Her wandering eyes took in the dozen benches and the few rude, heavy chairs which completed the rough furnishings of this rough room, and she shuddered. One little foot tapped sullenly upon the disordered floor which was littered with a miscellany of rushes interspread with such bones and scraps of food as the dogs had rejected or overlooked.

But to none of these surroundings did Bertrade de Montfort give but passing heed; she looked for the man she sought that she might quickly have the encounter over and learn what fate the future held in store for her.

Her quick glance had shown her that the room was quite empty, and that in addition to the main doorway at the lower end of the apartment, where she had entered, there was but one other door leading from the hall. This was at one side, and as it stood ajar she could see that it led into a small room, apparently a bedchamber.

As she stood facing the main doorway a panel opened quietly behind her and directly back of where the thrones had stood in past times. From the black mouth of the aperture stepped Peter of Colfax. Silently he closed the panel after him, and with soundless steps advanced toward the girl. At the edge of the raised dais he halted, rattling his sword to attract her attention.

If his aim had been to unnerve her by the suddenness and mystery of his appearance he failed signally, for she did not even turn her head as she said:

"What explanation hast thou to make, Sir Peter, for this base treachery against thy neighbor's daughter and thy sovereign's niece?"

"When fond hearts be thwarted by a cruel parent," replied the pot-bellied old beast in a soft and fawning tone, "love must still find its way; and so thy gallant swain hath dared the wrath of thy great father and majestic uncle, and lays his heart at thy feet, O beauteous Bertrade, knowing full well that thine hath been hungering after it since we didst first avow our love to thy hard hearted sire. See I kneel to thee, my dove!" And with cracking joints the fat baron plumped down upon his marrow bones.

Bertrade turned and as she saw him her haughty countenance relaxed into a sneering smile.

"Thou art a fool, Sir Peter," she said, "and, at that, the worst species of fool—an ancient fool. It is useless to pursue thy cause, for I will have none of thee. Let me hence, if thou be a gentleman, and no word of what hath transpired shall ever pass my lips. But let me go, 'tis all I ask, and it is useless to detain me for I cannot give what you would have. I do not love you, nor ever can I."

Her first words had caused the red of humiliation to mottle his already ruby visage to a semblance of purple, and now, as he attempted to rise with dignity he was still further covered with confusion by the fact that his huge stomach made it necessary for him to go upon all fours before he could rise, so that he got up much after the manner of a cow, raising his stern high in air in a most ludicrous fashion. As he gained his feet he saw the girl turn her head from him to hide the laughter on her face.

"Return to thy chamber," he thundered. "I will give thee until tomorrow to decide whether thou wilt accept Peter of Colfax as thy husband, or take another position in his household which will bar thee for all time from the society of thy kind."

The girl turned toward him, the laugh still playing on her lips.

"I will be wife to no buffoon; to no clumsy old clown; to no debauched, degraded parody of a man. And as for thy other rash threat, thou hast not the guts to put thy wishes into deeds, thou craven coward, for well ye know that Simon de Montfort would cut out thy foul heart with his own hand if he ever suspected thou wert guilty of speaking of such to me, his daughter." And Bertrade de Montfort swept from the great hall, and mounted to her tower chamber in the ancient Saxon stronghold of Colfax.

The old woman kept watch over her during the night and until late the following afternoon, when Peter of Colfax summoned his prisoner before him once more. So terribly had the old hag played upon the girl's fears that she felt fully certain that the Baron was quite equal to his dire threat, and so she had again been casting about for some means of escape or delay.

The room in which she was imprisoned was in the west tower of the castle, fully a hundred feet above the moat, which the single embrasure overlooked. There was, therefore, no avenue of escape in this direction. The solitary door was furnished with huge oaken bars, and itself composed of mighty planks of the same wood, cross barred with iron.

If she could but get the old woman out, thought Bertrade, she could barricade herself within and thus delay, at least, her impending fate in the hope that succor might come from some source. But her most subtle wiles proved ineffectual in ridding her, even for a moment, of her harpy jailer; and now that the final summons had come she was beside herself for a lack of means to thwart her captor.

Her dagger had been taken from her, but one hung from the girdle of the old woman and this Bertrade determined to have.

Feigning trouble with the buckle of her own girdle she called upon the old woman to aid her, and as the hag bent her head close to the girl's body to see what was wrong with the girdle clasp, Bertrade reached quickly to her side and snatched the weapon from its sheath. Quickly she sprang back from the old woman who, with a cry of anger and alarm, rushed upon her.

"Back!" cried the girl. "Stand back, old hag, or thou shalt feel the length of thine own blade."

The woman hesitated and then fell to cursing and blaspheming in a most horrible manner, at the same time calling for help.

Bertrade backed to the door, commanding the old woman to remain where she was, on pain of death, and quickly dropped the mighty bars into place. Scarcely had the last great bolt been slipped than Peter of Colfax with a dozen servants and men-at-arms were pounding loudly upon the outside.

"What's wrong within, Coll," cried the Baron.

"The wench has wrested my dagger from me and is murdering me," shrieked the old woman.

"An' that I will truly do, Peter of Colfax," spoke Bertrade, "if you do not immediately send for my friends to conduct me from thy castle, for I will not step my foot from this room until I know that mine own people stand without."

Peter of Colfax pled and threatened, commanded and coaxed, but all in vain. So passed the afternoon, and as darkness settled upon the castle the Baron desisted from his attempts, intending to starve his prisoner out.

Within the little room Bertrade de Montfort sat upon a bench guarding her prisoner, from whom she did not dare move her eyes for a single second. All that long night she sat thus, and when morning dawned it found her position unchanged, her tired eyes still fixed upon the hag.

Early in the morning Peter of Colfax resumed his endeavors to persuade her to come out; he even admitted defeat and promised her safe conduct to her father's castle, but Bertrade de Montfort was not one to be fooled by his lying tongue.

"Then will I starve you out," he cried at length.

"Gladly will I starve in preference to falling into thy foul hands," replied the girl. "But thy old servant here will starve first, for she be very old and not so strong as I. Therefore how will it profit you to kill two and still be robbed of thy prey?"

Peter of Colfax entertained no doubt but that his fair prisoner would carry out her threat and so he set his men to work with cold chisels, axes and saws upon the huge door.

For hours they labored upon that mighty work of defence, and it was late at night ere they made a little opening large enough to admit a hand and arm, but the first one intruded within the room to raise the bars was drawn quickly back with a howl of pain from its owner. Thus the keen dagger in the girl's hand put an end to all hopes of entering without completely demolishing the door.

To this work the men without then set themselves diligently while Peter of Colfax renewed his entreaties, through the small opening they had made. Bertrade replied but once.

"Seest thou this poniard?" she asked. "When that door falls this point enters my heart. There is nothing beyond that door, with thou, poltroon, to which death in this little chamber would not be preferable."

As she spoke she turned toward the man she was addressing, for the first time during all those weary, hideous hours removing her glance from the old hag. It was enough. Silently, but with the quickness of a tigress the old woman was upon her back, one claw-like paw grasping the wrist which held the dagger.

"Quick, My Lord!" she shrieked, "the bolts, quick."

Instantly Peter of Colfax ran his arm through the tiny opening in the door and a second later four of his men rushed to the aid of the old woman.

Easily they wrested the dagger from Bertrade's fingers, and at the Baron's bidding they dragged her to the great hall below.

As his retainers left the room at his command Peter of Colfax strode back and forth upon the rushes which strewed the floor. Finally he stopped before the girl standing rigid in the center of the room.

"Hast come to thy senses yet, Bertrade de Montfort?" he asked angrily. "I have offered you your choice; to be the honored wife of Peter of Colfax, or, by force, his mistress. The good priest waits without, what be your answer now?"

"The same as it has been these past two days," she replied with haughty scorn. "The same that it shall always be. I will be neither wife nor mistress to a coward; a hideous, abhorrent pig of a man. I would die, it seems, if I felt the touch of your hand upon me. You do not dare to touch me, you craven. I, the daughter of an earl, the niece of a king, wed to the warty toad, Peter of Colfax!"

"Hold, chit!" cried the Baron, livid with rage. "You have gone too far. Enough of this; and you love me not now I shall learn you to love ere the sun rises." And with a vile oath he grasped the girl roughly by the arm, and dragged her toward the little doorway at the side of the room.

CHAPTER X

FOR three weeks after his meeting with Bertrade de Montfort and his sojourn at the castle of John de Stutevill, Norman of Torn was busy with his wild horde in reducing and sacking the castle of John de Grey, a royalist baron who had captured and hanged two of the outlaw's fighting men; and never again after his meeting with the daughter of the chief of the barons did Norman of Torn raise a hand against the rebels or their friends.

Shortly after his return to Torn, following the successful outcome of his expedition, the watch upon the tower reported the approach of a dozen armed knights. Norman sent Red Shandy to the outer walls to learn the mission of the party, for visitors seldom came to this inaccessible and unhospitable fortress; and he well knew that no party of a dozen knights would venture with hostile intent within the clutches of his great band of villains.

The great red giant soon returned to say that it was Henry de Montfort, oldest son of the Earl of Leicester, who had come under a flag of truce and would have speech with the master of Torn.

"Admit them, Shandy," commanded Norman of Torn, "I will speak with them here."

When the party, a few moments later, was ushered into his presence it found itself facing a mailed knight with drawn visor.

116

Henry de Montfort advanced with haughty dignity until he faced the outlaw.

"Be ye Norman of Torn?" he asked. And did he try to conceal the hatred and loathing which he felt, he was poorly successful.

"They call me so," replied the visored knight. "And what may bring a De Montfort after so many years to visit his old neighbor?"

"Well ye know what brings me, Norman of Torn," replied the young man. "It is useless to waste words, and we cannot resort to arms, for you have us entirely in your power. Name your price and it shall be paid, only be quick and let me hence with my sister."

"What wild words be these, Henry de Montfort? Your sister! What mean you?"

"Yes, my sister Bertrade whom you stole upon the highroad two days since, after murdering the knights of John de Stutevill who were fetching her home from a visit upon the Baron's daughter. We know that it was you for the foreheads of the dead men bore your devil's mark."

"Shandy!" roared Norman of Torn. "*What means this?* Who has been upon the road, attacking women, in my absence? You were here and in charge during my visit to my Lord de Grey. As you value your hide, Shandy, the truth!"

"Since you laid me low in the hut of the good priest I have served you well, Norman of Torn; you should know my loyalty by this time and that never have I lied to you. No man of yours has done this thing, nor is it the first time that vile scoundrels have placed your mark upon their dead that they might thus escape suspicion, themselves."

"Henry de Montfort," said Norman of Torn, turning to his visitor, "we of Torn bear no savory name, that I know full well, but no man may say that we unsheath our swords against women. Your sister is not here. I give you the word of honor of Norman of Torn. Is it not enough?"

"They say you never lie," replied De Montfort. "Would to God I knew who had done this thing, or which way to search for my sister."

Norman of Torn made no reply, his thoughts were in wild confusion, and it was with difficulty that he hid the fierce anxiety of his heart or his rage against the perpetrators of this dastardly act which tore his whole being.

In silence De Montfort turned and left, nor had his party scarce passed the drawbridge ere the castle of Torn was filled with hurrying men and the noise and uproar of a sudden call to arms.

Some thirty minutes later five hundred iron clad horses carried their mailed riders beneath the portcullis of the grim pile, and Norman the Devil, riding at their head, spurred rapidly in the direction of the castle of Peter of Colfax.

The great troop, winding down the rocky trail from Torn's buttressed gates, presented a picture of wild barbaric splendor.

The armor of the men was of every style and metal, from the ancient banded mail of the Saxon to the richly ornamented plate armor of Milan. Gold and silver and precious stones set in plumed crest and breastplate and shield, and even in the steel spiked chamfrons of the horses' head armor showed the rich loot which had fallen to the portion of Norman of Torn's wild raiders.

Fluttering pennons streamed from five hundred lance points, and the gray banner of Torn, with the black falcon's wing, flew above each of the five companies. The great linden wood shields of the men were covered with gray leather and in the upper right hand corner of each was the black falcon's wing. The surcoats of the riders were also uniform, being of dark gray villosa faced with black wolf skin, so that notwithstanding the richness of the armor and the horse trappings there was a grim, gray warlike appearance to these wild companies that comported well with their reputation.

Recruited from all ranks of society and from every civilized country of Europe the great horde of Torn numbered in its ten companies serf and noble; Britain, Saxon, Norman, Dane, German, Italian and French, Scot, Pict and Irish.

Here birth caused no distinctions; the escaped serf, with the gall marks of his brass collar still visible about his neck, rode shoulder to shoulder with the outlawed scion of a noble house. The only requisites for admission to the troop were willingness and ability to fight, and an oath to obey the laws made by Norman of Torn.

The little army was divided into ten companies of one hundred men, each company captained by a fighter of proven worth and ability.

Our old friends Red Shandy, and John and James Flory led the first three companies, the remaining seven being under command of other seasoned veterans of a thousand fights.

One Eye Kanty, owing to his early trade, held the always important post of chief armorer, while Peter the Hermit, the last of the five cut-throats whom Norman of Torn had bested that day, six years before, in the hut of Father Claude, had become major-domo of the great castle of Torn, which post included also the vital functions of quartermaster and commissary.

The old man of Torn attended to the training of serf and squire in the art of war, for it was ever necessary to fill the gaps made in the companies, due to their constant encounters upon the highroad and their battles at the taking of some feudal castle; in which they did not always come off unscathed, though usually victorious.

Today, as they wound west across the valley, Norman of Torn rode at the head of the cavalcade, which strung out behind him in a long column. Above his gray steel armor a falcon's wing rose from his crest. It was the insignia which always marked him to his men in the midst of battle. Where it waved might always be found the fighting and the honors, and about it they were wont to rally.

Beside Norman of Torn rode the grim, gray, old man, silent and taciturn; nursing his deep hatred in the depths of his malign brain.

At the head of their respective companies rode the five captains: Red Shandy; John Flory; Edwild the Serf;

Emilio, Count de Gropello of Italy; and Sieur Ralph de la Campnee, of France.

The hamlets and huts which they passed in the morning and early afternoon brought forth men, women and children to cheer and wave God-speed to them; but as they passed farther from the vicinity of Torn where the black falcon wing was known more by the ferocity of its name than by the kindly deeds of the great outlaw to the lowly of his neighborhood, they saw only closed and barred doors with an occasional frightened face peering from a tiny window.

It was midnight ere they sighted the black towers of Colfax silhouetted against the starry sky. Drawing his men into the shadows of the forest a half mile from the castle, Norman of Torn rode forward with Shandy and some fifty men to a point as close as they could come without being observed. Here they dismounted and Norman of Torn crept stealthily forward alone.

Taking advantage of every cover he approached to the very shadows of the great gate without being detected. In the castle a light shone dimly from the windows of the great hall, but no other sign of life was apparent. To his intense surprise, Norman of Torn found the drawbridge lowered and no sign of watchmen at the gate or upon the walls.

As he had sacked this castle some two years since he was familiar with its internal plan, and so he knew that through the scullery he could reach a small antechamber above, which let directly into the great hall.

And so it happened that as Peter of Colfax wheeled toward the door of the little room he stopped short in terror, for there before him stood a strange knight in armor, with lowered visor and drawn sword. The girl saw him too, and a look of hope and renewed courage o'erspread her face.

"Draw!" commanded a low voice in English, "unless you prefer to pray, for you are about to die."

"Who be ye, varlet?" cried the Baron. "Ho, John! Ho, Guy! To the rescue, quick!" he shrieked, and drawing his sword he attempted to back quickly toward the main doorway of the hall; but the man in armor was upon him and forcing him to fight ere he had taken three steps.

It had been short shrift for Peter of Colfax that night had not John and Guy and another of his henchmen rushed into the room with drawn swords.

"Ware! Sir Knight," cried the girl, as she saw the three knaves rushing to the aid of their master.

Turning to meet their assault the knight was forced to abandon the terror-stricken Baron for an instant, and again he had made for the doorway bent only on escape; but the girl had divined his intentions, and running quickly to the entrance she turned the great lock and threw the key with all her might to the far corner of the hall. In an instant she regretted her act, for she saw that where she might have reduced her rescuer's opponents by at least one she had now forced the cowardly Baron to remain, and nothing fights more fiercely than a cornered rat.

The knight was holding his own splendidly with the three retainers, and for an instant Bertrade de Montfort stood spell-bound by the exhibition of swordsmanship she was witnessing.

Fighting the three alternately, in pairs and again all at the same time the silent knight, though weighted by his heavy armor, forced them steadily back; his flashing blade seeming to weave a net of steel about them. Suddenly his sword stopped just for an instant, stopped in the heart of one of his opponents, and as the man lunged to the floor it was flashing again close to the breasts of the two remaining men-at-arms.

Another went down less than ten seconds later, and then the girl's attention was called to the face of the horrified Baron; Peter of Colfax was moving—slowly and cautiously, he was creeping, from behind, toward the visored knight, and in his raised hand flashed a thin sharp dagger.

For an instant the girl stood frozen with horror, unable to move a finger or to cry out; but only for an instant, and then, regaining control of her muscles, she stooped quickly and grasping a heavy foot-stool hurled it full at Peter of Colfax.

It struck him below the knees and toppled him to the floor just as the knight's sword passed through the throat of his final antagonist.

As the Baron fell he struck heavily upon a table which supported the only lighted cresset within the chamber. In an instant all was darkness. There was a rapid shuffling sound as of the scurrying of rats and then the quiet of the tomb settled upon the great hall.

"Are you safe and unhurt, my Lady Bertrade?" asked a grave English voice out of the darkness.

"Quite, Sir Knight," she replied, "and you?"

"Not a scratch, but where is our good friend the Baron?"

"He lay here upon the floor but a moment since, and carried a thin long dagger in his hand. Have a care, Sir Knight, he may even now be upon you."

The knight did not answer, but she heard him moving boldly about the room. Soon he had found another lamp and made a light. As its feeble rays slowly penetrated the black gloom the girl saw the bodies of the three men-at-arms, the overturned table and lamp, and the visored knight; but Peter of Colfax was gone.

The knight perceived his absence at the same time, but he only laughed a low, grim laugh.

"He will not go far, My Lady Bertrade," he said.

"How know you my name?" she asked. "Who may you be? I do not recognize your armor, and your breastplate bears no arms."

He did not answer at once and her heart rose in her breast as it filled with the hope that her brave rescurer might be the same Roger de Condé who had saved her from the hirelings of Peter of Colfax but a few short weeks since. Surely it was the same straight and mighty figure, and there was the marvelous sword play as well. It must be he, and yet Roger de Condé had spoken no English while this man spoke it well, though, it was true, with a slight French accent.

"My Lady Bertrade, I be Norman of Torn," said the visored knight with quiet dignity.

The girl's heart sank, and a feeling of cold fear crept through her. For years that name had been the symbol of fierce cruelty, and mad hatred against her kind. Little children were frightened into obedience by the vaguest hint that the Devil of Torn would get them, and grown men had come to whisper the name with grim, set lips.

"Norman of Torn!" she whispered. "May God have mercy on my soul!"

Beneath the visored helm a wave of pain and sorrow surged across the countenance of the outlaw, and a little shudder, as of a chill of hopelessness, shook his giant frame.

"You need not fear, My Lady," he said sadly. "You shall be in your father's castle of Leicester ere the sun marks noon. And you will be safer under the protection of the hated Devil of Torn than with your own mighty father, or your royal uncle."

"It is said that you never lie, Norman of Torn," spoke the girl, "and I believe you, but tell me why you thus befriend a De Montfort."

"It is not for love of your father or your brothers, nor yet hatred of Peter of Colfax, nor neither for any reward whatsoever. It pleases me to do as I do, that is all. Come."

He led her in silence to the courtyard and across the lowered drawbridge, to where they soon discovered a group of horsemen, and in answer to a low challenge from Shandy, Norman of Torn replied that it was he.

"Take a dozen men, Shandy, and search yon hellhole. Bring out to me, alive, Peter of Colfax, and My Lady's cloak and a palfrey—and Shandy, when all is done as I say, you may apply the torch! but no looting, Shandy."

Shandy looked in surprise upon his leader, for the torch had never been a weapon of Norman of Torn, while loot, if not always the prime object of his many raids, was at least a very important consideration.

The outlaw noticed the surprised hesitation of his faithful subaltern and signing him to listen, said:

"Red Shandy, Norman of Torn has fought and sacked and pillaged for the love of it, and for a principle which was at best but a vague generality. Tonight we ride to redress a wrong done to My Lady Bertrade de Montfort, and that, Shandy, is a different matter. The torch, Shandy, from tower to scullery, but in the service of My Lady, no looting."

"Yes, My Lord," answered Shandy, and departed with his little detachment.

In a half hour he returned with a dozen prisoners, but no Peter of Colfax.

"He has flown, My Lord," the big fellow reported, and indeed it was true. Peter of Colfax had passed through the vaults beneath his castle and by a long subterranean passage had reached the quarters of some priests without the lines of Norman of Torn. By this time he was several miles on his way to the coast, and France; for he had recognized the swordsmanship of the outlaw, and did not care to remain in England and face the wrath of both Norman of Torn and Simon de Montfort.

"He will return," was the outlaw's only comment, when he had been fully convinced that the Baron had escaped.

They watched until the castle had burst into flames in

a dozen places, the prisoners huddled together in terror and apprehension, fully expecting a summary and horrible death.

When Norman of Torn had assured himself that no human power could now save the doomed pile, he ordered that the march be taken up, and the warriors filed down the roadway behind their leader and Bertrade de Montfort, leaving their erstwhile prisoners sorely puzzled but unharmed and free.

As they looked back they saw the heavens red with the great flames that sprang high above the lofty towers. Immense volumes of dense smoke rolled southward across the sky line. Occasionally it would clear away from the burning castle for an instant to show the black walls pierced by their hundreds of embrasures, each lit up by the red of the raging fire within. It was a gorgeous, impressive spectacle, but one so common in those fierce, wild days, that none thought it worthy of more than a passing backward glance.

Varied emotions filled the breasts of the several riders who wended their slow way down the mud-slippery road. Norman of Torn was both elated and sad. Elated that he had been in time to save this girl who awakened such strange emotions in his breast; sad that he was a loathesome thing in her eyes. But that it was pure happiness just to be near her, sufficed him for the time; of the morrow, what use to think! The little, grim, gray, old man of Torn nursed the spleen he did not dare vent openly, and cursed the chance that had sent Henry de Montfort to Torn to search for his sister; while the followers of the outlaw swore quietly over the vagary which had brought them on this long ride without either fighting or loot.

Bertrade de Montfort was but filled with wonder that she should owe her life and honor to this fierce, wild cut-throat who had sworn especial hatred against her family, because of its relationship to the house of Plantagenet. She could not fathom it, and yet, he seemed fair spoken for so rough a man; she wondered what manner of countenance might lie beneath that barred visor.

Once the outlaw took his cloak from its fastenings at his saddle's cantel and threw it about the shoulders of the girl, for the night air was chilly, and again he dismounted and led her palfrey around a bad place in the road, lest the beast might slip and fall.

She thanked him in her courtly manner for these services, but beyond that no word passed between them, and they came, in silence, about midday within sight of the castle of Simon de Montfort.

The watch upon the tower was thrown into confusion by the approach of so large a party of armed men, so that, by the time they were in hailing distance, the walls of the great structure were crowded with fighting men.

Shandy rode ahead with a flag of truce, and when he was beneath the castle walls Simon de Montfort called forth:

"Who be ye and what your mission? Peace or war?"

"It is Norman of Torn, come in peace, and in the service of a De Montfort," replied Shandy. "He would enter with one companion, my Lord Earl."

"Dares Norman of Torn enter the castle of Simon

de Montfort—thinks he that I keep a robbers' roost!" cried the fierce old warrior.

"Norman of Torn dares ride where he will in all England," boasted the red giant. "Will you see him in peace, My Lord?"

"Let him enter," said De Montfort, "but no knavery, now, we are a thousand men here, well armed and ready fighters."

Shandy returned to his master with the reply, and together Norman of Torn and Bertrade de Montfort clattered across the drawbridge beneath the portcullis of the castle of the Earl of Leicester, brother-in-law of Henry III of England.

The girl was still wrapped in the great cloak of her protector, for it had been raining, so that she rode beneath the eyes of her father's men without being recognized. In the courtyard they were met by Simon de Montfort, and his sons Henry and Simon.

The girl threw herself impetuously from her mount, and, flinging aside the outlaw's cloak, rushed toward her astounded parent.

"What means this," cried De Montfort, "has the rascal offered you harm or indignity?"

"You craven liar," cried Henry de Montfort, "but yesterday you swore upon your honor that you did not hold my sister, and I, like a fool, believed." And with his words the young man flung himself upon Norman of Torn with drawn sword.

Quicker than the eye could see, the sword of the visored knight flew from its scabbard, and, with a single lightning-like move, sent the blade of young De

Montfort hurtling cross the courtyard; and then before either could take another step, Bertrade de Montfort had sprung between them and placing a hand upon the breastplate of the outlaw stretched forth the other with palm out-turned toward her kinsmen as though to protect Norman of Torn from further assault.

"Be he outlaw or devil," she cried, "he is a brave and courteous knight, and he deserves from the hands of the De Montforts the best hospitality they can give, and not cold steel and insults." Then she explained briefly to her astonished father and brothers what had befallen during the past few days.

Henry de Montfort, with the fine chivalry that marked him, was the first to step forward with outstretched hand to thank Norman of Torn, and to ask his pardon for his rude words and hostile act.

The outlaw but held up his open palm, as he said, "Let the De Montforts think well ere they take the hand of Norman of Torn. I give not my hand except in friendship, and not for a passing moment; but for life. I appreciate your present feelings of gratitude, but let them not blind you to the fact that I am still Norman the Devil, and that you have seen my mark upon the brows of your dead. I would gladly have your friendship, but I wish it for the man, Norman of Torn, with all his faults as well as what virtues you may think him to possess."

"You are right, sir," said the Earl, "you have our gratitude and our thanks for the service you have rendered the house of Montfort, and ever during our lives you may command our favors. I admire your bravery and your candor, but while you continue the Outlaw of Torn you may not break bread at the table of De Montfort as a friend would have the right to do."

"Your speech is that of a wise and careful man," said Norman of Torn quietly. "I go, but remember that from this day I have no quarrel with the House of Simon de Montfort, and that should you need my arms they are at your service, a thousand strong. Goodbye." But as he turned to go, Bertrade de Montfort confronted him with outstretched hand.

"You must take my hand in friendship," she said, "for to my dying day I must ever bless the name of Norman of Torn because of the horror from which he has rescued me."

He took the little fingers in his mailed hand, and bending upon one knee raised them to his lips.

"To no other—woman, man, king, God, or devil—has Norman of Torn bent the knee. If ever you need him, My Lady Bertrade, remember that his services are yours for the asking."

And turning he mounted and rode in silence from the courtyard of the castle of Leicester. Without a backward glance, and with his five hundred men at his back, Norman of Torn disappeared beyond a turning in the roadway.

"A strange man," said Simon de Montfort, "both good and bad, but from today I shall ever believe more good than bad. Would that he were other than he be for his arm would wield a heavy sword against the enemies of England, an he could be persuaded to our cause."

"Who knows," said Henry de Montfort, "but that an offer of friendship might have won him to a better life. It seemed that in his speech was a note of wistfulness. I wish, father, that we had taken his hand."

CHAPTER XI

SEVERAL days after Norman of Torn's visit to the castle of Leicester, a young knight appeared before the Earl's gates demanding admittance to have speech with Simon de Montfort. The Earl received him, and as the young man entered his presence Simon de Montfort sprang to his feet in astonishment.

"My Lord Prince," he cried. "What do ye here, and alone?"

The young man smiled.

"I be no prince, My Lord," he said, "though some have said that I favor the King's son. I be Roger de Condé whom it may have pleased your gracious daughter to mention. I have come to pay homage to Bertrade de Montfort."

"Ah," said De Montfort, rising to greet the young knight cordially, "an you be that Roger de Condé who rescued my daughter from the fellows of Peter of Colfax, the arms of the De Montforts are open to you.

"Bertrade has had your name upon her tongue many times since her return. She will be glad indeed to receive you, as is her father. She has told us of your valiant espousal of her cause, and the thanks of her brothers and mother await you, Roger de Condé.

"She also told us of your strange likeness to Prince Edward, but until I saw you I could not believe two men could be born of different mothers and yet be so identical. Come, we will seek out my daughter and her mother."

De Montfort led the young man to a small chamber where they were greeted by Princess Eleanor, his wife, and by Bertrade de Montfort. The girl was frankly glad to see him once more and laughingly chid him because he had allowed another to usurp his prerogative and rescue her from Peter of Colfax.

"And to think," she cried, "that it should have been Norman of Torn who fulfilled your duties for you. But he did not capture Sir Peter's head, my friend; that is still at large to be brought to me upon a golden dish."

"I have not forgotten, Lady Bertrade," said Roger de Condé. "Peter of Colfax will return."

The girl glanced at him quickly.

"The very words of the Outlaw of Torn," she said. "How many men be ye, Roger de Condé? With raised visor you could pass in the King's court for the King's son; and in manner, and form, and swordsmanship, and your visor lowered, you might easily be hanged for Norman of Torn."

"And which would it please ye most that I be?" he laughed.

"Neither," she answered, "I be satisfied with my friend, Roger de Condé."

"So ye like not the Devil of Torn?" he asked.

"He has done me a great service, and I be under monstrous obligations to him, but he be, nathless, the Outlaw of Torn and I the daughter of an earl and a king's sister."

"A most unbridgeable gulf indeed," commented Roger de Condé, drily. "Not even gratitude could lead a king's niece to receive Norman of Torn on a footing of equality."

"He has my friendship, always," said the girl, "but I doubt me if Norman of Torn be the man to impose upon it."

"One can never tell," said Roger de Condé, "what manner of fool a man may be. When a man's head be filled with a pretty face, what room be there for reason?"

"Soon thou wilt be a courtier, if thou keep long at this turning of pretty compliments," said the girl coldly; "and I like not courtiers, nor their empty, hypocritical chatter."

The man laughed.

"If I turned a compliment I did not know it," he said. "What I think, I say. It may not be a courtly speech or it may. I know nothing of courts and care less, but be it man or maid to whom I speak, I say what is in my mind or I say nothing. I did not in so many words say that you are beautiful, but I think it nevertheless, and ye cannot be angry with my poor eyes if they deceive me into believing that no fairer woman breathes the air of England. Nor can you chide my sinful brain that it gladly believes what mine eyes tell it. No, you may not be angry so long as I do not tell you all this."

Bertrade de Montfort did not know how to answer so ridiculous a sophistry; and, truth to tell, she was more than pleased to hear from the lips of Roger de Condé what bored her on the tongues of other men.

De Condé was the guest of the Earl of Leicester

for several days, and before his visit was terminated the young man had so won his way into the good graces of the family that they were loath to see him leave.

Although denied the society of such as these throughout his entire life, yet it seemed that he fell as naturally into the ways of their kind as though he had always been among them. His starved soul, groping through the darkness of the empty past, yearned toward the feasting and the light of friendship, and urged him to turn his back upon the old life, and remain ever with these people, for Simon de Montfort had offered the young man a position of trust and honor in his retinue.

"Why refused you the offer of my father?" said Bertrade to him as he was come to bid her farewell. "Simon de Montfort is as great a man in England as the King himself, and your future were assured did you attach your self to his person. But what am I saying! Did Roger de Condé not wish to be elsewhere he had accepted, and as he did not accept it is proof positive that he does not wish to bide among the De Montforts."

"I would give my soul to the devil," said Norman of Torn, "would it buy me the right to remain ever at the feet of Bertrade Montfort."

He raised her hand to his lips in farewell as he started to speak, but something—was it an almost imperceptible pressure of her little fingers, a quickening of her breath or a swaying of her body toward him?—caused him to pause and raise his eyes to hers.

For an instant they stood thus, the eyes of the man sinking deep into the eyes of the maid, and then hers closed and with a little sigh that was half gasp she swayed toward him, and the Devil of Torn folded the King's niece in his mighty arms and his lips placed the seal of a great love upon those that were upturned to him.

The touch of those pure lips brought the man to himself.

"Ah, Bertrade, my Bertrade," he cried, "what is this thing that I have done! Forgive me, and let the greatness and the purity of my love for you plead in extenuation of my act."

She looked up into his face in surprise, and then placing her strong white hands upon his shoulders, she whispered:

"See, Roger, I am not angry. It is not wrong that we love; tell me it is not, Roger."

"You must not say that you love me, Bertrade. I am a coward, a craven poltroon; but, God, how I love you."

"But," said the girl, "I do love—"

"Stop," he cried, "not yet, not yet. Do not say it till I come again. You know nothing of me, you do not know even who I be; but when next I come I promise that ye shall know as much of me as I myself know, and then, Bertrade, my Bertrade, if you can then say, 'I love you' no power on earth, or in heaven above, or hell below shall keep you from being mine!"

"I will wait, Roger, for I believe in you and trust you. I do not understand, but I know that you must have some good reason, though it all seems very strange to me. If I, a De Montfort, am willing to acknowledge my love for any man there can be no reason why I should not do so, unless," and she started at the sudden thought, wide-eyed and paling, "unless there be another woman, a—a—wife?"

"There is no other woman, Bertrade," said Norman of Torn. "I have no wife; nor within the limits of my memory have my lips ever before touched the lips of another, for I do not remember my mother."

She sighed a happy little sigh of relief, and laughing lightly, said:

"It is some old woman's bugaboo that you are haling out of a dark corner of your imagination to frighten yourself with. I do not fear, since I know that you must be all good. There be no line of vice or deception upon your face and you are very brave. So brave and noble a man, Roger, has a heart of pure gold."

"Don't," he said, bitterly. "I cannot endure it. Wait until I come again and then, oh my flower of all England, if you have it in your heart to speak as you are speaking now the sun of my happiness will be at zenith. Then, but not before, shall I speak to the Earl, thy father. Farewell, Bertrade, in a few days I return."

"If you would speak to the Earl on such a subject, you insolent young puppy, you may save your breath," thundered an angry voice, and Simon de Montfort strode, scowling, into the room.

The girl paled, but not from fear of her father, for the fighting blood of the De Montforts was as strong in her as in her sire. She faced him with as brave and resolute a face as did the young man, who turned slowly, fixing De Montfort with level gaze.

"I heard enough of your words as I was passing through the corridor," continued the latter, "to readily guess what had gone before. So it is for this that you have wormed your sneaking way into my home? And thought you that Simon de Montfort would throw his daughter at the head of the first passing rogue? Who be ye, but a nameless rascal? For aught we know some low born lackey. Get ye hence, and be only thankful that I do not aid you with the toe of my boot where it would do the most good."

"Stop!" cried the girl. "Stop, father, hast forgot that but for Roger de Condé ye might have seen your daughter a corpse ere now, or, worse, herself befouled and dishonored?"

"I do not forget," replied the Earl, "and it is because I remember, that my sword remains in its scabbard. The fellow has been amply repaid by the friendship of De Montfort, but now this act of perfidy has wiped clean the score. An' you would go in peace, sirrah, go quickly, ere I lose my temper."

"There has been some misunderstanding on your part, My Lord," spoke Norman of Torn, quietly and without apparent anger or excitement. "Your daughter has not told me that she loves me, nor did I contemplate asking you for her hand. When next I come, first shall I see her and if she will have me, My Lord, I shall come to you to tell you that I shall wed her. Norm —Roger de Condé asks permission of no man to do what he would do."

Simon de Montfort was fairly bursting with rage but he managed to control himself to say,

"My daughter weds whom I select, and even now I have practically closed negotiations for her betrothal to

Prince Philip, nephew of King Louis of France. And as for you, sir, I would as lief see her the wife of the Outlaw of Torn. He at least has wealth and power, and a name that be known outside his own armor. But enough of this; get you gone, nor let me see your face again within the walls of Leicester's castle."

"You are right, My Lord, it were foolish and idle for us to be quarreling with words," said the outlaw. "Farewell, My Lady. I shall return as I promised, and your word shall be law." And with a profound bow to De Montfort, Norman of Torn left the apartment, and in a few minutes was riding through the courtyard of the castle toward the main portals.

As he passed beneath a window in the castle wall a voice called to him from above, and drawing in his horse, he looked up into the eyes of Bertrade de Montfort.

"Take this, Roger de Condé," she whispered, dropping a tiny parcel to him, "and wear it ever, for my sake. We may never meet again, for the Earl, my father, is a mighty man, not easily turned from his decisions; therefore I shall say to you, Roger de Condé, what you forbid my saying, I love you, and be ye prince or scullion you may have me, if you can find the means to take me."

"Wait, my lady, until I return, then shall you decide and if ye be of the same mind as today, never fear but that I shall take ye. Again, farewell." And with a brave smile that hid a sad heart, Norman of Torn passed out of the castle yard.

When he undid the parcel which Bertrade had tossed

to him he found that it contained a beautifully wrought ring set with a single opal.

The Outlaw of Torn raised the little circlet to his lips, and then slipped it upon the third finger of his left hand.

CHAPTER XII

NORMAN of Torn did not return to the castle of Leicester "in a few days," nor for many months. For news came to him that Bertrade de Montfort had been posted off to France in charge of her mother.

From now on the forces of Torn were employed in repeated attacks on royalist barons, encroaching ever and ever southward until even Berkshire and Surrey and Sussex felt the weight of the iron hand of the outlaw.

Nearly a year had elapsed since that day when he had held the fair form of Bertrade de Montfort in his arms, and in all that time he had heard no word from her.

He would have followed her to France but for the fact that, after he had parted from her and the intoxication of her immediate presence had left his brain clear to think rationally, he had realized the futility of his hopes, and he had seen that the pressing of his suit could mean only suffering and mortification for the woman he loved.

His better judgment told him that she, on her part, when freed from the subtle spell woven by the nearness and the newness of a first love would doubtless be glad to forget the words she had spoken in the heat of a divine passion. He would wait, then, until fate threw them together, and should that ever chance, while she was still free, he would let her know that

Roger de Condé and the Outlaw of Torn were one and the same.

If she wants me then, he thought, but she will not, no it is impossible. It is better that she marry her French prince than to live, dishonored, the wife of a common highwayman; for though she might love me at first, the bitterness and loneliness of her life would turn her love to hate.

As the outlaw was sitting one day in the little cottage of Father Claude, the priest reverted to the subject of many past conversations; the unsettled state of civil conditions in the realm, and the stand which Norman of Torn would take when open hostilities between King and baron were declared.

"It would seem that Henry," said the priest, "by his continued breaches of both the spirit and letter of the Oxford Statutes is but urging the barons to resort to arms; and the fact that he virtually forced Prince Edward to take up arms against Humphrey de Bohun last fall, and to carry the ravages of war throughout the Welsh border provinces, convinces me that he be by this time well equipped to resist De Montfort and his associates."

"If that be the case," said Norman of Torn, "we shall have war and fighting in real earnest ere many months."

"And under which standard does My Lord Norman expect to fight?" asked Father Claude.

"Under the black falcon's wing," laughed he of Torn.

"Thou be indeed a close-mouthed man, my son," said the priest, smiling. "Such an attribute helpeth make a great statesman. With thy soldierly qualities in addition, my dear boy, there be a great future for thee in the paths of honest men. Dost remember our past talk?"

"Yes, father, well; and often have I thought on't. I have one more duty to perform here in England and then it may be, that I shall act on thy suggestion, but only on one condition."

"What be that, my son?"

"That wheresoere I go thou must go also. Thou be my best friend; in truth, my father; none other have I ever known, for the little old man of Torn, even though I be the product of his loins, which I much mistrust, be no father to me."

The priest sat looking intently at the young man for many minutes before he spoke.

Without the cottage a swarthy figure skulked beneath one of the windows, listening to such fragments of the conversation within as came to his attentive ears. It was Spizo the Spaniard. He crouched entirely concealed by a great lilac bush, which many times before had hid his traitorous form.

At length the priest spoke.

"Norman of Torn," he said, "so long as thou remain in England, pitting thy great host against the Plantagenet King and the nobles and barons of his realm, thou be but serving as the cats-paw of another. Thyself hast said an hundred times that thou knowst not the reason for thy hatred against them. Thou be too strong a man to so throw thy life uselessly away to satisfy the choler of another.

"There be that of which I dare not speak to thee yet and only may I guess and dream of what I think, nor do I know whether I must hope that it be false or true, but now, if ever, the time hath come for the question to be settled. Thou hast not told me in so many words, but I be an old man and versed in reading true between the lines, and so I know that thou lovest Bertrade de Montfort. Nay, do not deny it. And now what I would say be this. In all England there lives no more honorable man than Simon de Montfort, nor none who could more truly decide upon thy future and thy past. Thou may not understand of what I hint, but thou know that thou may trust me, Norman of Torn."

"Yea, even with my life and honor, my father," replied the outlaw.

"Then promise me that with the old man of Torn alone thou wilt come hither when I bidst thee and meet Simon de Montfort, and abide by his decision should my surmises concerning thee be correct. He will be the best judge of any in England, save two who must now remain nameless."

"I will come, Father, but it must be soon for on the fourth day we ride south."

"It shall be by the third day, or not at all," replied Father Claude, and Norman of Torn rising to leave wondered at the moving leaves of the lilac bush without the window, for there was no breeze.

Spizo the Spaniard reached Torn several minutes before the outlaw chief and had already poured his tale into the ears of the little, grim, gray, old man.

As the priest's words were detailed to him the old man of Torn paled in anger.

"The fool priest will upset the whole work to which

I have devoted near twenty years," he muttered, "if I find not the means to quiet his half-wit tongue. Between priest and petticoat it be all but ruined now. Well then, so much the sooner must I act, and I know not but that now be as good a time as any. If we come near enough to the King's men on this trip south, the gibbet shall have its own and a Plantagenet dog shall taste the fruits of his own tyranny," then glancing up and realizing that Spizo the Spaniard had been a listener, the old man, scowling, cried:

"What said I, sirrah? What didst hear?"

"Naught, My Lord; thou didst but mutter incoherently," replied the Spaniard.

The old man eyed him closely.

"An did I more, Spizo, thou heardst naught but muttering, remember."

"Yes, My Lord."

An hour later the old man of Torn dismounted before the cottage of Father Claude and entered.

"I am honored," said the priest, rising.

"Priest," cried the old man, coming immediately to the point, "Norman of Torn tells me that thou wish him and me and Leicester to meet here. I know not what thy purpose may be, but for the boy's sake carry not out thy design as yet. I may not tell thee my reasons, but it be best that this meeting take place after we return from the south."

The old man had never spoken so fairly to Father Claude before, and so the latter was quite deceived and promised to let the matter rest until later.

A few days after, in the summer of 1263, Norman of Torn rode at the head of his army of outlaws through the county of Essex, down toward London town. One thousand fighting men there were, with squires and other servants, and five hundred sumpter beasts to transport their tents and other impedimenta, and bring back the loot.

But a small force of ailing men-at-arms, and servants had been left to guard the castle of Torn under the able direction of Peter the Hermit.

At the column's head rode Norman of Torn and the little grim, gray, old man; and behind them nine companies of knights, followed by the catapult detachment; then came the sumpter beasts. Horsan the Dane, with his company, formed the rear guard. Three hundred yards in advance of the column rode ten men to guard against surprise and ambuscades.

The pennons, and the banners and the bugles; and the loud rattling of sword, and lance and armor and iron-shod hoof carried to the eye and ear ample assurance that this great cavalcade of iron men was bent upon no peaceful mission.

All his captains rode today with Norman of Torn. Beside those whom we have met there was Don Piedro Castro y Pensilo of Spain; Baron of Cobarth of Germany, and Sir John Mandecote of England. Like their leader, each of these fierce warriors carried a great price upon his head, and the story of the life of any one would fill a large volume with romance, war, intrigue, treachery, bravery and death.

Toward noon one day in the midst of a beautiful

valley of Essex they came upon a party of ten knights escorting two young women. The meeting was at a turn in the road, so that the two parties were upon each other before the ten knights had an opportunity to escape with their fair wards.

"What the devil be this," cried one of the knights, as the main body of the outlaw horde came into view, "the King's army or one of his foreign legions?"

"It be Norman of Torn and his fighting men," replied the outlaw.

The faces of the knights blanched, for they were ten against a thousand, and there were two women with them.

"Who be ye?" said the outlaw.

"I am Richard de Tany of Essex," said the oldest knight, he who had first spoken, "and these be my daughter and her friend, Mary de Stutevill. We are upon our way from London to my castle. What would you of us? Name your price, if it can be paid with honor it shall be paid; only let us go our way in peace. We cannot hope to resist the Devil of Torn, for we be but ten lances. If ye must have blood, at least let the women go unharmed."

"My Lady Mary is an old friend," said the outlaw. "I called at her father's home but little more than a year since. We are neighbors, and the lady can tell you that women are safer at the hands of Norman of Torn than they might be in the King's palace."

"Right he is," spoke up Lady Mary, "Norman of Torn accorded my mother, my sister, and myself the utmost respect; though I cannot say as much for his treatment of my father," she added, half smiling.

"I have no quarrel with you, Richard de Tany," said Norman of Torn. "Ride on."

The next day a young man hailed the watch upon the walls of the castle of Richard de Tany telling him to bear word to Joan de Tany that Roger de Condé, a friend of her guest Lady Mary de Stutevill, was without.

In a few moments the great drawbridge sank slowly into place and Norman of Torn trotted into the courtyard.

He was escorted to an apartment where Mary de Stutevill and Joan de Tany were waiting to receive him. Mary de Stutevill greeted him as an old friend, and the daughter of de Tany was no less cordial in welcoming her friend's friend to the hospitality of her father's castle.

"Are all your old friends and neighbors come after you to Essex," cried Joan de Tany, laughingly, addressing Mary. "Today it is Roger de Condé, yesterday it was the Outlaw of Torn. Methinks Derby will soon be depopulated unless you return quickly to your home."

"I rather think it be for news of another that we owe this visit from Roger de Condé," said Mary, smiling. "For I have heard tales, and I see a great ring upon the gentleman's hand—a ring which I have seen before."

Norman of Torn made no attempt to deny the reason for his visit, but asked bluntly if she heard aught of Bertrade de Montfort.

"Thrice within the year have I received missives from her," replied Mary. "In the first two she spoke only of Roger de Condé, wondering why he did not come to France after her; but in the last she mentions not his name, but speaks of her approaching marriage with Prince Philip."

Both girls were watching the countenance of Roger de Condé narrowly, but no sign of the sorrow which filled his heart showed itself upon his face.

"I guess it be better so," he said quietly. "The daughter of a De Montfort could scarcely be happy with a nameless adventurer," he added, a little bitterly.

"You wrong her, my friend," said Mary de Stutevill, "she loved you, and unless I know not the friend of my childhood as well as I know myself, she loves you yet; but Bertrade de Montfort is a proud woman and what can you expect when she hears no word from you for a year? Thought you that she would seek you out and implore you to rescue her from the alliance her father has made for her?"

"You do not understand," he answered, "and I may not tell you; but I ask that you believe me when I say that it was for her own peace of mind, for her own happiness, that I did not follow her to France. But let us talk of other things; the sorrow is mine and I would not force it upon others. I cared only to know that she is well, and, I hope, happy. It will never be given to me to make her or any other woman so. I would that I had never come into her life, but I did not know what I was doing; and the spell of her beauty and goodness was strong upon me, so that I was weak and could not resist what I had never known before in all my life— love."

"You could not well be blamed," said Joan de Tany, generously. "Bertrade de Montfort is all and even more than you have said; it be a benediction simply to have known her."

As she spoke, Norman of Torn looked upon her critically for the first time, and he saw that Joan de Tany was beautiful, and that when she spoke her face lighted with a hundred little changing expressions of intelligence and character that cast a spell of fascination about her. Yes, Joan de Tany was good to look upon, and Norman of Torn carried a wounded heart in his breast that longed for surcease from its sufferings—for a healing balm upon its hurts and bruises.

And so it came to pass that for many days the Outlaw of Torn was a daily visitor at the castle of Richard de Tany, and the acquaintance between the man and the two girls ripened into a deep friendship, and with one of them it threatened even more.

Norman of Torn, in his ignorance of the ways of women, saw only friendship in the little acts of Joan de Tany. His life had been a hard and lonely one. The only ray of brilliant and warming sunshine that had entered it had been his love for Bertrade de Montfort and hers for him.

His every thought was loyal to the woman whom he knew was not for him, but he longed for the companionship of his own kind and so welcomed the friendship of such as Joan de Tany and her fair guest. He did not dream that either looked upon him with any warmer sentiment than the sweet friendliness which was as new to him as love—how could he mark the line between or foresee the terrible price of his ignorance!

Mary de Stutevill saw and she thought the man but fickle and shallow in matters of the heart—many there were, she knew, who were thus. She might have warned him had she known the truth, but instead she let things drift except for a single word of warning to Joan de Tany.

"Be careful of thy heart, Joan," she said, "lest it be getting away from thee into the keeping of one who seems to love no less quickly than he forgets."

The daughter of De Tany flushed.

"I am quite capable of safeguarding my own heart, Mary de Stutevill," she replied warmly. "If thou covet this man thyself, why, but say so—do not think though that because thy heart glows in his presence mine is equally susceptible."

It was Mary's turn now to show offense, and a sharp retort was on her tongue when suddenly she realized the folly of such a useless quarrel. Instead she put her arms about Joan and kissed her.

"I do not love him," she said, "and I be glad that you do not, for I know that Bertrade does, and that but a short year since he swore undying love for her. Let us forget that we have spoken on the subject."

It was at this time that the King's soldiers were harassing the lands of the rebel barons, and taking a heavy toll in revenge for their stinging defeat at Rochester earlier in the year, so that it was scarcely safe for small parties to venture upon the roadways lest they fall into the hands of the mercenaries of Henry III.

Not even were the wives and daughters of the barons exempt from the attacks of the royalists; and it was no uncommon occurrence to find them suffering imprisonment, and something worse, at the hands of the King's supporters.

And in the midst of these alarms it entered the willful head of Joan de Tany that she wished to ride to London town and visit the shops of the merchants.

While London itself was solidly for the barons and against the King's party, the road between the castle of Richard de Tany and the city of London was beset with many dangers.

"Why," cried the girl's mother in exasperation, "between robbers and royalists and the Outlaw of Torn you would not be safe if you had an army to escort you."

"But then, as I have no army," retorted the laughing girl, "if you reason by your own logic, I shall be indeed quite safe."

And when Roger de Condé attempted to dissuade her, she taunted him with being afraid of meeting with the Devil of Torn, and told him that he might remain at home and lock himself safely in her mother's pantry.

And so, as Joan de Tany was a spoiled child, they set out upon the road to London; the two girls with a dozen servants and knights; and Roger de Condé was of the party.

At the same time a grim, gray, old man dispatched a messenger from the outlaw's camp; a swarthy fellow, disguised as a priest, whose orders were to proceed to London, and when he saw the party of Joan de Tany, with Roger de Condé, enter the city he was to deliver the letter he bore to the captain of the gate.

The letter contained this brief message:

"The tall knight in gray with closed helm is Norman of Torn," and was unsigned.

All went well and Joan was laughing merrily at the fears of those who had attempted to dissuade her when, at a cross road, they discovered two parties of armed men approaching from opposite directions. The leader of the nearer party spurred forward to intercept the little band, and, reining in before them, cried brusquely,

"Who be ye?"

"A party on a peaceful mission to the shops of London," replied Norman of Torn.

"I asked not your mission," cried the fellow. "I asked, who be ye? Answer, and be quick about it."

"I be Roger de Condé, gentleman of France, and these be my sisters and servants," lied the outlaw, "and were it not that the ladies be with me your answer would be couched in steel, as you deserve for your boorish insolence."

"There be plenty of room and time for that even now, you dog of a French coward," cried the officer, couching his lance as he spoke.

Joan de Tany was sitting her horse where she could see the face of Roger de Condé, and it filled her heart with pride and courage as she saw and understood the little smile of satisfaction that touched his lips as he heard the man's challenge and lowered the point of his own spear.

Wheeling their horses toward one another the two combatants, who were some ninety feet apart, charged at full tilt. As they came together the impact was so great that both horses were nearly overturned and the two powerful war lances were splintered into a hundred fragments as each struck the exact center of his opponent's shield. Then, wheeling their horses and throwing away the butts of their now useless lances, De Condé and the officer advanced with drawn swords.

The fellow made a most vicious return assault upon De Condé, attempting to ride him down in one mad rush, but his thrust passed harmlessly from the tip of the outlaw's sword, and as the officer wheeled back to renew the battle they settled down to fierce combat, their horses wheeling and turning shoulder to shoulder.

The two girls sat rigid in their saddles watching the encounter, the eyes of Joan de Tany alight with the fire of battle as she followed every move of the wondrous sword play of Roger de Condé.

He had not even taken the precaution to lower his visor, and the grim and haughty smile that played upon his lips spoke louder than many words the utter contempt in which he held the sword of his adversary. And as Joan de Tany watched she saw the smile suddenly freeze to a cold, hard line, and the eyes of the man narrow to mere slits, and her woman's intuition read the death warrant of the King's officer ere the sword of the outlaw buried itself in his heart.

The other members of the two bodies of royalist soldiers had sat spellbound as they watched the battle, but now, as their leader's corpse rolled from the saddle they spurred furiously in upon De Condé and his little party.

The Baron's men put up a noble fight, but the odds were heavy and even with the mighty arm of Norman of Torn upon their side the outcome was apparent from the first.

Five swords were flashing about the outlaw, but his blade was equal to the thrust and one after another of his assailants crumpled up in their saddles as his leaping point found their vitals.

Nearly all of the Baron's men were down, when one, an old servitor, spurred to the side of Joan de Tany and Mary de Stutevill.

"Come, my ladies," he cried, "quick and you may escape. They be so busy with the battle that they will never notice."

"Take the Lady Mary, John," cried Joan, "I brought Roger de Condé to this pass against the advice of all, and I remain with him to the end."

"But, My Lady—" cried John.

"But nothing, sirrah!" she interrupted sharply. "Do as you are bid. Follow my Lady Mary, and see that she comes to my father's castle in safety," and raising her riding whip she struck Mary's palfrey across the rump so that the animal nearly unseated his fair rider as he leaped frantically to one side and started madly up the road down which they had come.

"After her, John," commanded Joan peremptorily, "and see that you turn not back until she be safe within the castle walls; then you may bring aid."

The old fellow had been wont to obey the imperious

little Lady Joan from her earliest childhood, and the habit was so strong upon him that he wheeled his horse and galloped after the flying palfrey of the Lady Mary de Stutevill.

As Joan de Tany turned again to the encounter before her, she saw fully twenty men surrounding Roger de Condé, and while he was taking heavy toll of those before him he could not cope with the men who attacked him from behind; and even as she looked she saw a battle axe fall full upon his helm, and his sword drop from his nerveless fingers as his lifeless body rolled from the back of Sir Mortimer to the battle-tramped clay of the highroad.

She slid quickly from her palfrey and ran fearlessly toward his prostrate form, reckless of the tangled mass of snorting, trampling, steel-clad horses, and surging fighting-men that surrounded him. And well it was for Norman of Torn that this brave girl was there that day, for even as she reached his side the sword point of one of the soldiers was at his throat for the *coup de grace*.

With a cry Joan de Tany threw herself across the outlaw's body, shielding him as best she could from the threatening sword.

Cursing loudly, the soldier grasped her roughly by the arm to drag her from his prey, but at this juncture a richly armored knight galloped up and drew rein beside the party.

The newcomer was a man of about forty-five or fifty; tall, handsome, black-mustached and with the haughty arrogance of pride most often seen upon the faces of those who have been raised by unmerited favor to positions of power and affluence.

He was John de Fulm, Earl of Buckingham, a foreigner by birth and for years one of the King's favorites; the bitterest enemy of De Montfort and the barons.

"What now?" he cried. "What goes on here?"

The soldiers fell back, and one of them replied:

"A party of the King's enemies attacked us, My Lord Earl, but we routed them, taking these two prisoners."

"Who be ye?" he said, turning toward Joan who was kneeling beside De Condé, and as she raised her head, "My God! The daughter of De Tany! a noble prize indeed my men. And who be the knight?"

"Look for yourself, My Lord Earl," replied the girl removing the helm, which she had been unlacing from the fallen man.

"Edward?" he ejaculated. "But no, it cannot be, I did but yesterday leave Edward in Dover."

"I know not who he be," said Joan de Tany, "except that he be the most marvelous fighter and the bravest man it has ever been given me to see. He called himself Roger de Condé, but I know nothing of him other than—that he looks like a prince, and fights like a devil. I think he has no quarrel with either side, My Lord, and so, as you certainly do not make war on women, you will let us go our way in peace as we were when your soldiers wantonly set upon us."

"A De Tany, madam, were a great and valuable capture in these troublous times," replied the Earl, "and that alone were enough to necessitate my keeping you; but a beautiful De Tany is yet a different matter and so I will grant you at least one favor, I will not take you to the King, but a prisoner you shall be in mine own castle for I am alone, and need the cheering company of a fair and loving lady."

The girl's head went high as she looked the Earl full in the eye.

"Think you, John de Fulm, Earl of Buckingham, that you be talking to some comely scullery maid? Do you forget that my house is honored in England, even though it does not share the King's favors with his foreign favorites, and you owe respect to a daughter of a De Tany?"

"All be fair in war, my beauty," replied the Earl. "Egad," he continued, "methinks all would be fair in hell were they like unto you. It has been some years since I have seen you and I did not know the old fox Richard de Tany kept such a package as this hid in his grimy old castle."

"Then you refuse to release us?" said Joan de Tany.

"Let us not put it thus harshly," countered the Earl. "Rather let us say that it be so late in the day, and the way so beset with dangers that the Earl of Buckingham could not bring himself to expose the beautiful daughter of his old friend to the perils of the road, and so—"

"Let us have an end to such foolishness," cried the girl. "I might have expected naught better from a turncoat foreign knave such as thee, who once joined in the councils of De Montfort, and then betrayed his friends to curry favor with the King."

The Earl paled with rage, and pressed forward as

159

though to strike the girl, but thinking better of it, he turned to one of the soldiers, saying:

"Bring the prisoner with you. If the man lives bring him also. I would learn more of this fellow who masquerades in the countenance of a crown prince."

And turning, he spurred on towards the neighboring castle of a rebel baron which had been captured by the royalists, and was now used as headquarters by De Fulm.

CHAPTER XIII

WHEN Norman of Torn regained his senses he found himself in a small tower room in a strange castle. His head ached horribly, and he felt sick and sore; but he managed to crawl from the cot on which he lay, and by steadying his swaying body with hands pressed against the wall he was able to reach the door. To his disappointment he found this locked from without, and in his weakened condition he made no attempt to force it.

He was fully dressed and in armor, as he had been when struck down, but his helmet was gone, as were also his sword and dagger.

The day was drawing to a close, and as dusk fell and the room darkened he became more and more impatient. Repeated pounding upon the door brought no response and finally he gave up in despair. Going to the window he saw that his room was some thirty feet above the stone-flagged courtyard, and also that it looked at an angle upon other windows in the old castle where lights were beginning to show. He saw men-at-arms moving about, and once he thought he caught a glimpse of a woman's figure, but he was not sure.

He wondered what had become of Joan de Tany and Mary de Stutevill. He hoped that they had escaped, and yet—no, Joan certainly had not, for now he distinctly remembered that his eyes had met hers for an instant just before the blow fell upon him, and he thought of the faith and confidence that he had read in that quick glance. Such a look would nerve a jackal to attack a drove of lions, thought the outlaw. What a beautiful creature she was; and she had stayed there with him during the fight. He remembered now; Mary de Stutevill had not been with her as he had caught that glimpse of her, no, she had been all alone. Ah! That was friendship indeed!

What else was it that tried to force its way above the threshold of his bruised and wavering memory? Words? Words of love? And lips pressed to his? No, it must be but a figment of his wounded brain.

What was that which clicked against his breastplate? He felt, and found a metal bauble linked to a mesh of his steel armor by a strand of silken hair. He carried the little thing to the window, and in the waning light made it out to be a golden hair ornament set with precious stones, but he could not tell if the little strand of silken hair were black or brown. Carefully he detached the little thing, and, winding the filmy tress about it, placed it within the breast of his tunic. He was vaguely troubled by it, yet why he could scarcely have told, himself.

Again turning to the window he watched the lighted rooms within his vision, and presently his view was rewarded by the sight of a knight coming within the scope of the narrow casement of a nearby chamber.

From his apparel he was a man of position, and he was evidently in heated discussion with some one whom Norman of Torn could not see. The man, a great,

,tall black-haired and mustached nobleman, was pounding upon a table to emphasize his words, and presently he sprang up as though rushing toward the one to whom he had been speaking. He disappeared from the watcher's view for a moment and then, at the far side of the apartment, Norman of Torn saw him again just as he roughly grasped the figure of a woman who evidently was attempting to escape him. As she turned to face her tormentor all the devil in the Devil of Torn surged in his aching head, for the face he saw was that of Joan de Tany.

With a muttered oath the imprisoned man turned to hurl himself against the bolted door, but ere he had taken a single step the sound of heavy feet without brought him to a stop, and the jingle of keys as one was fitted to the lock of the door sent him gliding stealthily to the wall beside the doorway, where the inswinging door would conceal him.

As the door was pushed back a flickering torch lighted up, but dimly, the interior, so that until he had reached the center of the room, the visitor did not see that the cot was empty.

He was a man-at-arms, and at his side hung a sword. That was enough for the Devil of Torn—it was a sword he craved most; and, ere the fellow could assure his slow wits that the cot was empty, steel fingers closed upon his throat, and he went down beneath the giant form of the outlaw.

Without other sound than the scuffing of their bodies on the floor, and the clanking of their armor, they fought, the one to reach the dagger at his side, the other to close forever the windpipe of his adversary.

Presently the man-at-arms found what he sought, and, after tugging with ever diminishing strength, he felt the blade slip from its sheath. Slowly and feebly he raised it high above the back of the man on top of him; with a last supreme effort he drove the point downward, but ere it reached its goal there was a sharp snapping sound as of a broken bone, the dagger fell harmlessly from his dead hand, and his head rolled backward upon his broken neck.

Snatching the sword from the body of his dead antagonist, Norman of Torn rushed from the tower room.

As John de Fulm, Earl of Buckingham, laid his vandal hands upon Joan de Tany she turned upon him like a tigress. Blow after blow she rained upon his head and face until, in mortification and rage, he struck her full upon the mouth with his clenched fist; but even this did not subdue her and with ever weakening strength she continued to strike him. And then the great royalist Earl, the chosen friend of the King, took the fair white throat between his great fingers, and the lust of blood supplanted the lust of love, for he would have killed her in his rage.

It was upon this scene that the Outlaw of Torn burst with naked sword. They were at the far end of the apartment, and his cry of anger at the sight caused the Earl to drop his prey, and turn with drawn sword to meet him.

There were no words, for there was no need of words

here. The two men were upon each other, and fighting to the death, before the girl had regained her feet. It would have been short shrift for John de Fulm had not some of his men heard the fracas, and rushed to his aid.

Four of them there were, and they tumbled pell-mell into the room, fairly falling upon Norman of Torn in their anxiety to get their swords into him; but once they met that master hand they went more slowly, and in a moment two of them went no more at all, and the others, with the Earl, were but circling warily in search of a chance opening—an opening which never came.

Norman of Torn stood with his back against a table in an angle of the room, and behind him stood Joan de Tany.

"Move toward the left," she whispered. "I know this old pile. When you reach the table that bears the lamp there will be a small doorway directly behind you, strike the lamp out with your sword, as you feel my hand in your left, and then I will lead you through that doorway, which you must turn and quickly bolt after us. Do you understand?"

He nodded.

Slowly he worked his way toward the table, the men-at-arms in the meantime keeping up an infernal howling for help. The Earl was careful to keep out of reach of the point of De Condé's sword, and the men-at-arms were nothing loath to emulate their master's example.

Just as he reached his goal a dozen more men burst into the room, and emboldened by this reinforcement one of the men engaging De Condé came too close. As he jerked his blade from the fellow's throat, Norman of Torn felt a firm, warm hand slipped into his from behind, and his sword swung with a resounding blow against the lamp.

As darkness enveloped the chamber Joan de Tany led him through the little door, which he immediately closed and bolted as she had instructed.

"This way," she whispered, again slipping her hand into his, and in silence she led him through several dim chambers, and finally stopped before a blank wall in a great oak-panelled room.

Here the girl felt with swift fingers the edge of the molding; more and more rapidly she moved as the sound of hurrying footsteps resounded through the castle.

"What is wrong?" asked Norman of Torn, noticing her increasing perturbation.

"*Mon Dieu!*" she cried. "Can I be wrong! Surely this is the room. Oh, my friend, that I should have brought you to all this by my willfulness and vanity; and now when I might save you my wits leave me and I forget the way."

"Do not worry about me," laughed the Devil of Torn. "Methought that it was I who was trying to save you, and may heaven forgive me else, for surely that be my only excuse for running away from a handful of swords. I could not take chances when thou wert at stake, Joan," he added more gravely.

The sound of pursuit was now quite close, in fact

the reflection from flickering torches could be seen in nearby chambers.

At last the girl, with a little cry of "stupid," seized De Condé and rushed him to the far side of the room.

"Here it is," she whispered joyously, "here it has been all the time." Running her fingers along the molding until she found a little hidden spring she pushed it, and one of the great panels swung slowly in, revealing the yawning mouth of a black opening behind.

Quickly the girl entered, pulling De Condé after her, and as the panel swung quietly into place the Earl of Buckingham with a dozen men entered the apartment.

"The devil take them," cried De Fulm. "Where can they have gone? Surely we were right behind them."

"It is passing strange, My Lord," replied one of the men. "Let us try the floor above, and the towers; for of a surety they have not come this way." And the party retraced its steps, leaving the apartment empty.

Behind the panel the girl stood shrinking close to De Condé, her hand still in his.

"Where now?" he asked. "Or do we stay hidden here like frightened chicks until the war is over and the Baron returns to let us out of this musty hole?"

"Wait," she answered, "until I quiet my nerves a little. I am all unstrung." He felt her body tremble as it pressed against his.

With the spirit of protection strong within him what wonder that his arm fell about her shoulder as though to say, fear not, for I be brave and powerful; naught can harm you while I am here.

Presently she reached her hands up to his face, made brave to do it by the sheltering darkness.

"Roger," she whispered, her tongue halting over the familiar name. "I thought that they had killed you, and all for me, for my foolish stubbornness. Canst forgive me?"

"Forgive?" he asked, smiling to himself. "Forgive being given an opportunity to fight? There be nothing to forgive, Joan, unless it be that I should ask forgiveness for protecting thee so poorly."

"Do not say that," she commanded. "Never was such bravery or such swordsmanship in all the world before; never such a man."

He did not answer. His mind was a chaos of conflicting thoughts. The feel of her hands as they had lingered momentarily, and with a vague caress upon his cheek, and the pressure of her body as she leaned against him sent the hot blood coursing through his veins. He was puzzled, for he had not dreamed that friendship was so sweet. That she did not shrink from his encircling arms should have told him much, but Norman of Torn was slow to realize that a woman might look upon him with love. Nor had he a thought of any other sentiment toward her than that of friend and protector.

And then there came to him as in a vision another fair and beautiful face—Bertrade de Montfort's—and Norman of Torn was still more puzzled; for at heart he was clean, and love of loyalty was strong within him. Love of women was a new thing to him, and, robbed as he had been all his starved life of the affection and kindly fellowship, of either men or women, it is little to be wondered at that he was easily impressionable and responsive to the feeling his strong personality had awakened in two of England's fairest daughters.

But with the vision of that other face there came to him a faint realization that mayhap it was a stronger power than either friendship or fear which caused that lithe, warm body to cling so tightly to him. That the responsibility for the critical stage their young acquaintance had so quickly reached was not his had never for a moment entered his head. To him the fault was all his; and perhaps it was this quality of chivalry that was the finest of the many noble characteristics of his sterling character. So his next words were typical of the man; and did Joan de Tany love him, or did she not, she learned that night to respect and trust him as she respected and trusted few men of her acquaintance.

"My Lady," said Norman of Torn, "we have been through much, and we are as little children in a dark attic, and so if I have presumed upon our acquaintance," and he lowered his arm from about her shoulder, "I ask you to forgive it for I scarce know what to do, from weakness and from the pain of the blow upon my head."

Joan de Tany drew slowly away from him, and without reply took his hand and led him forward through a dark, cold corridor.

"We must go carefully now," she said at last, "for there be stairs near."

He held her hand pressed very tightly in his, tighter

perhaps than conditions required, but she let it lie
there as she led him forward, very slowly down a flight
of rough stone steps.

Norman of Torn wondered if she were angry with
him and then, being new at love, he blundered.

"Joan de Tany," he said.

"Yes, Roger de Condé; what would you?"

"You be silent, and I fear that you be angry with
me. Tell me that you forgive what I have done, an it
offended you. I have so few friends," he added sadly,
"that I cannot afford to lose such as you."

"You will never lose the friendship of Joan de Tany,"
she answered. "You have won her respect and—and—"
But she could not say it and so she trailed off lamely—
"and undying gratitude."

But Norman of Torn knew the word that she would
have spoken had he dared to let her. He did not, for
there was always the vision of Bertrade de Montfort
before him; and now another vision arose that would
effectually have sealed his lips had not the other—he
saw the Outlaw of Torn dangling by his neck from a
wooden gibbet.

Before, he had only feared that Joan de Tany loved
him, now he knew it, and while he marvelled that so
wondrous a creature could feel love for him, again he
blamed himself, and felt sorrow for them both; for
he did not return her love nor could he imagine a love
strong enough to survive the knowledge that it was
possessed by the Devil of Torn.

Presently they reached the bottom of the stairway,
and Joan de Tany led him, gropingly, across what

seemed, from their echoing footsteps, a large chamber. The air was chill and dank, smelling of mold, and no ray of light penetrated this subterranean vault, and no sound broke the stillness.

"This be the castle's crypt," whispered Joan; "and they do say that strange happenings occur here in the still watches of the night, and that when the castle sleeps the castle's dead rise from their coffins and shake their dry bones.

"Sh! what was that?" as a rustling noise broke upon their ears close upon their right; and then there came a distinct moan, and Joan de Tany fled to the refuge of Norman of Torn's arms.

"There is nothing to fear, Joan," reassured Norman of Torn. "Dead men wield not swords, nor do they move, or moan. The wind, I think, and rats are our only companions here."

"I am afraid," she whispered. "If you can make a light I am sure you will find an old lamp here in the crypt, and then will it be less fearsome. As a child I visited this castle often, and in search of adventure we passed through these corridors an hundred times, but always by day and with lights."

Norman of Torn did as she bid, and finding the lamp, lighted it. The chamber was quite empty save for the coffins in their niches, and some effigies in marble set at intervals about the walls."

"Not such a fearsome place after all," he said, laughing lightly.

"No place would seem fearsome now," she answered

simply, "were there a light to show me that the brave face of Roger de Condé were by my side."

"Hush, child," replied the outlaw. "You know not what you say. When you know me better you will be sorry for your words, for Roger de Condé is not what you think him. So say no more of praise until we be out of this hole, and you safe in your father's halls."

The fright of the noises in the dark chamber had but served to again bring the girl's face close to his so that he felt her hot, sweet breath upon his cheek, and thus another link was forged to bind him to her.

With the aid of the lamp they made more rapid progress, and in a few moments reached a low door at the end of the arched passageway.

"This is the doorway which opens upon the ravine below the castle. We have passed beneath the walls and the moat. What may we do now, Roger, without horses?"

"Let us get out of this place, and as far away as possible under the cover of darkness, and I doubt not I may find a way to bring you to your father's castle," replied Norman of Torn.

Putting out the light, lest it should attract the notice of the watch upon the castle walls, Norman of Torn pushed open the little door and stepped forth into the fresh night air.

The ravine was so overgrown with tangled vines and wildwood that had there ever been a pathway it was now completely obliterated; and it was with difficulty that the man forced his way through the entangling creepers and tendrils. The girl stumbled after him and twice fell before they had taken a score of steps.

"I fear I am not strong enough," she said finally. "The way is much more difficult than I had thought."

So Norman of Torn lifted her in his strong arms, and stumbled on through the darkness and the shrubbery down the center of the ravine. It required the better part of an hour to traverse the little distance to the roadway; and all the time her head nestled upon his shoulder and her hair brushed his cheek. Once when she lifted her head to speak to him he bent toward her, and in the darkness, by chance, his lips brushed hers. He felt her little form tremble in his arms, and a faint sigh breathed from her lips.

They were upon the highroad now, but he did not put her down. A mist was before his eyes, and he could have crushed her to him and smothered those warm lips with his own. Slowly his face inclined toward hers, closer and closer his iron muscles pressed her to him, and then, clear cut and distinct before his eyes, he saw the corpse of the Outlaw of Torn swinging by the neck from the arm of a wooden gibbet, and beside it knelt a woman gowned in rich cloth of gold and many jewels. Her face was averted and her arms were outstretched toward the dangling form that swung and twisted from the grim, gaunt arm. Her figure was racked with choking sobs of horror-stricken grief. Presently she staggered to her feet and turned away, burying her face in her hands; but he saw her features for an instant then—the woman who openly and alone mourned the dead Outlaw of Torn was Bertrade de Montfort.

Slowly his arms relaxed, and gently and reverently he lowered Joan de Tany to the ground. In that instant Norman of Torn had learned the difference between friendship and love, and love and passion.

The moon was shining brightly upon them, and the girl turned, wide-eyed and wondering, toward him. She had felt the wild call of love and she could not understand his seeming coldness now, for she had seen no vision beyond a life of happiness within those strong arms.

"Joan," he said, "I would but now have wronged thee. Forgive me. Forget what has passed between us until I can come to you in my rightful colors, when the spell of the moonlight and adventure be no longer upon us, and then,"—he paused—"and then I shall tell you who I be and you shall say if you still care to call me friend—no more than that shall I ask."

He had not the heart to tell her that he loved only Bertrade de Montfort, but it had been a thousand times better had he done so.

She was about to reply when a dozen armed men sprang from the surrounding shadows, calling upon them to surrender. The moonlight falling upon the leader revealed a great giant of a fellow with an enormous, bristling mustache—it was Shandy.

Norman of Torn lowered his raised sword.

"It is I, Shandy," he said. "Keep a still tongue in thy head until I speak with thee apart. Wait here, My Lady Joan; these be friends."

Drawing Shandy to one side he learned that the faithful fellow had become alarmed at his chief's continued absence, and had set out with a small party to search for him. They had come upon the riderless Sir Mortimer grazing by the roadside, and a short distance beyond had discovered evidences of the conflict at the cross-roads. There they had found Norman of Torn's helmet, confirming their worst fears. A peasant in a nearby hut had told them of the encounter, and had set them upon the road taken by the Earl and his prisoners.

"And here we be, My Lord," concluded the great fellow.

"How many are you?" asked the outlaw.

"Fifty, all told, with those who lie farther back in the bushes."

"Give us horses, and let two of the men ride behind us," said the chief. "And, Shandy, let not the lady know that she rides this night with the Outlaw of Torn."

"Yes, My Lord."

They were soon mounted, and clattering down the road, back toward the castle of Richard de Tany.

Joan de Tany looked in silent wonder upon this grim force that sprang out of the shadows of the night to do the bidding of Roger de Condé, a gentleman of France.

There was something familiar in the great hulk of Red Shandy; where had she seen that mighty frame before? And now she looked closely at the figure of Roger de Condé. Yes, somewhere else had she seen these two men together; but where and when?

And then the strangeness of another incident came

175

to her mind. Roger de Condé spoke no English, and yet she had plainly heard English words upon this man's lips as he addressed the red giant.

Norman of Torn had recovered his helmet from one of his men who had picked it up at the cross-roads, and now he rode in silence with lowered visor, as was his custom.

There was something sinister now in his appearance, and as the moonlight touched the hard, cruel faces of the grim and silent men who rode behind him, a little shudder crept over the frame of Joan de Tany.

Shortly before daylight they reached the castle of Richard de Tany, and a great shout went up from the watch as Norman of Torn cried:

"Open! Open for My Lady Joan."

Together they rode into the courtyard, where all was bustle and excitement. A dozen voices asked a dozen questions only to cry out still others without waiting for replies.

Richard de Tany with his family and Mary de Stute-vill were still fully clothed, having not lain down during the whole night. They fairly fell upon Joan and Roger de Condé in their joyous welcome and relief.

"Come, come," said the Baron, "let us go within. You must be fair famished for good food and drink."

"I will ride, My Lord," replied Norman of Torn. "I have a little matter of business with my friend the Earl of Buckingham. Business which I fear will not wait."

Joan de Tany looked on in silence. Nor did she urge him to remain, as he raised her hand to his lips in farewell. So Norman of Torn rode out of the courtyard; and as his men fell in behind him under the first rays of the drawing day, the daughter of De Tany watched them through the gate, and a great light broke upon her, for what she saw was the same as she had seen a few days since when she had turned in her saddle to watch the retreating forms of the cut-throats of Torn as they rode on after halting her father's party.

CHAPTER XIV

SOME hours later fifty men followed Norman of Torn on foot through the ravine below the castle where John de Fulm, Earl of Buckingham, had his headquarters; while nearly a thousand more lurked in the woods before the grim pile.

Under cover of the tangled shrubbery they crawled unseen to the little door through which Joan de Tany had led him the night before. Following the corridors and vaults beneath the castle they came to the stone stairway, and mounted to the passage which led to the false panel that had given the two fugitives egress.

Slipping the spring lock, Norman of Torn entered the apartment followed closely by his henchmen. On they went, through apartment after apartment, but no sign of the Earl or his servitors rewarded their search, and it was soon apparent that the castle was deserted.

As they came forth into the courtyard they descried an old man basking in the sun, upon a bench. The sight of them nearly caused the old fellow to die of fright, for to see fifty armed men issue from the untenanted halls was well reckoned to blanch even a braver cheek.

When Norman of Torn questioned him he learned that De Fulm had ridden out early in the day bound for Dover, where Prince Edward then was. The outlaw knew it would be futile to pursue him, but yet, so fierce was his anger against this man, that he ordered his band to mount, and spurring to their head, he marched through Middlesex, and crossing the Thames above London, entered Surrey late the same afternoon.

As they were going into camp that night in Kent, midway between London and Rochester, word came to Norman of Torn that the Earl of Buckingham, having sent his escort on to Dover, had stopped to visit the wife of a royalist baron, whose husband was with Prince Edward's forces.

The fellow who gave this information was a servant in my lady's household who held a grudge against his mistress for some wrong she had done him. When, therefore, he found that these grim men were searching for De Fulm he saw a way to be revenged upon his mistress.

"How many swords be there at the castle?" asked Norman of Torn.

"Scarce a dozen, barring the Earl of Buckingham," replied the knave; "and, furthermore, there be a way to enter, which I may show you, My Lord, so that you may, unseen, reach the apartment where My Lady and the Earl be supping."

"Bring ten men, beside yourself, Shandy," commanded Norman of Torn. "We shall pay a little visit upon our amorous friend, My Lord, the Earl of Buckingham."

Half an hour's ride brought them within sight of the castle. Dismounting, and leaving their horses with one of the men, Norman of Torn advanced on foot with

Shandy and the eight others, close in the wake of the traitorous servant.

The fellow led them to the rear of the castle, where, among the brush, he had hidden a rude ladder, which, when tilted, spanned the moat and rested its farther end upon a window ledge some ten feet above the ground.

"Keep the fellow here till last, Shandy," said the outlaw, "till all be in, an' if there be any signs of treachery stick him through the gizzard—death thus be slower and more painful."

So saying Norman of Torn crept boldly across the improvised bridge, and disappeared within the window beyond. One by one the band of cut-throats passed through the little window, until all stood within the castle beside their chief; Shandy coming last with the servant.

"Lead me quietly, knave, to the room where My Lord sups," said Norman of Torn. "You, Shandy, place your men where they can prevent my being interrupted."

Following a moment or two after Shandy came another figure stealthily across the ladder, and as Norman of Torn and his followers left the little room this figure pushed quietly through the window and followed the great outlaw down the unlighted corridor.

A moment later My Lady of Leybourn looked up from her plate upon the grim figure of an armored knight standing in the doorway of the great dining hall.

"My Lord Earl!" she cried. "Look! behind you."

And as the Earl of Buckingham glanced behind him

he overturned the bench upon which he sat, in his effort to gain his feet; for My Lord Earl of Buckingham had a guilty conscience.

The grim figure raised a restraining hand, as the Earl drew his sword.

"A moment, My Lord," said a low voice in perfect French.

"Who are you?" cried the lady.

"I be an old friend of My Lord, here; but let me tell you a little story.

"In a grim old castle in Essex, only last night, a great lord of England held by force the beautiful daughter of a noble house, and, when she spurned his advances, he struck her with his clenched fist upon her fair face, and with his brute hands choked her. And in that castle also was a despised and hunted outlaw, with a price upon his head, for whose neck the hempen noose has been yawning these many years. And it was this vile person who came in time to save the young woman from the noble flower of knighthood that would have ruined her young life.

"The outlaw wished to kill the knight, but many men-at-arms came to the noble's rescue, and so the outlaw was forced to fly with the girl lest he be overcome by numbers, and the girl thus fall again into the hands of her tormentor.

"But this crude outlaw was not satisfied with merely rescuing the girl, he must needs mete out justice to her noble abductor and collect in full the toll of blood which alone can atone for the insult and violence done her.

"My Lady, the young girl was Joan de Tany; the noble was My Lord the Earl of Buckingham; and the outlaw stands before you to fulfill the duty he has sworn to do. *En garde*, My Lord!"

The encounter was short, for Norman of Torn had come to kill, and he had been looking through a haze of blood for hours—in fact every time he had thought of those brutal fingers upon the fair throat of Joan de Tany and of the cruel blow that had fallen upon her face.

He showed no mercy, but backed the Earl relentlessly into a corner of the room, and when he had him there where he could escape in no direction, he drove his blade so deep through his putrid heart that the point buried itself an inch in the oak panel beyond.

Claudia Leybourn sat frozen with horror at the sight she was witnessing, and, as Norman of Torn wrenched his blade from the dead body before him and wiped it on the rushes of the floor, she gazed in awful fascination while he drew his dagger and made a mark upon the forehead of the dead nobleman.

"Outlaw or Devil," said a stern voice behind them, "Roger Leybourn owes you his friendship for saving the honor of his home."

Both turned to discover a mail-clad figure standing in the doorway where Norman of Torn had first appeared.

"Roger!" shrieked Claudia Leybourn, and swooned.

"Who be you?" continued the master of Leybourn addressing the outlaw.

For answer Norman of Torn pointed to the forehead

of the dead Earl of Buckingham, and there Roger Leybourn saw, in letters of blood, NT.

The Baron advanced with outstretched hand.

"I owe you much, you have saved my poor, silly wife from this beast, and Joan de Tany is my cousin, so I am doubly beholden to you, Norman of Torn."

The outlaw pretended that he did not see the hand.

"You owe me nothing, Sir Roger, that may not be paid by a good supper; I have eaten but once in forty-eight hours."

The outlaw now called to Shandy and his men, telling them to remain on watch, but to interfere with no one within the castle.

He then sat at the table with Roger Leybourn and his lady, who had recovered from her swoon, and behind them on the rushes of the floor lay the body of De Fulm in a little pool of blood.

Leybourn told them that he had heard that De Fulm was at his home, and had hastened back; having been in hiding about the castle for half an hour before the arrival of Norman of Torn, awaiting an opportunity to enter unobserved by the servants. It was he who had followed across the ladder after Shandy.

The outlaw spent the night at the castle of Roger Leybourn; for the first time within his memory a welcomed guest under his true name at the house of a gentleman.

The following morning he bade his host goodbye, and returning to his camp started on his homeward march toward Torn.

Near midday, as they were approaching the Thames

near the environs of London, they saw a great concourse of people hooting and jeering at a small party of gnetlemen and gentlewomen.

Some of the crowd were armed, and from very force of numbers were waxing brave to lay violent hands upon the party. Mud and rocks and rotten vegetables were being hurled at the little cavalcade, many of them barely missing the women of the party.

Norman of Torn waited to ask no questions, but spurring into the thick of it laid right and left of him with the flat of his sword, and his men, catching the contagion of it, swarmed after him until the whole pack of attacking ruffians were driven into the Thames.

And then, without a backward glance at the party he had rescued, he continued on his march toward the north.

The little party sat upon their horses looking in wonder after the retreating figures of their deliverers. Then one of the ladies turned to a knight at her side with a word of command and an imperious gesture toward the fast disappearing company. He thus addressed put spurs to his horse, and rode at a rapid gallop after the outlaw's troop. In a few moments he had overtaken them and reined up beside Norman of Torn.

"Hold, Sir Knight," cried the gentleman, "the Queen would thank you in person for your brave defence of her."

Ever keen to see the humor of a situation, Norman of Torn wheeled his horse and rode back with the Queen's messenger.

As he faced Her Majesty the Outlaw of Torn bent low over his pommel.

"You be a strange knight that thinks so lightly on saving a queen's life that you ride on without turning your head, as though you had but driven a pack of curs from annoying a stray cat," said the Queen.

"I drew in the service of a woman, Your Majesty, not in the service of a queen."

"What now! Wouldst even belittle the act which we all witnessed? The King, my husband, shall reward thee, Sir Knight, if you but tell me your name."

"If I told my name methinks the King would be more apt to hang me," laughed the outlaw. "I be Norman of Torn."

The entire party looked with startled astonishment upon him, for none of them had ever seen this bold raider whom all the nobility and gentry of England feared and hated.

"For lesser acts than that which thou hast just perfored, the King has pardoned men before," replied Her Majesty. "But raise your visor, I would look upon the face of so notorious a criminal who can yet be a gentleman and a loyal protector of his queen."

"They who have looked upon my face, other than my friends," replied Norman of Torn quietly, "have never lived to tell what they saw beneath this visor; and as for you, Madame, I have learned within the year to fear it might mean unhappiness to you to see the visor of the Devil of Torn lifted from his face." Without another word he wheeled and galloped back to his little army.

"The puppy, the insolent puppy," cried Eleanor of England, in a rage.

And so the Outlaw of Torn and his mother met and parted after a period of twenty years.

Two days later Norman of Torn directed Red Shandy to lead to forces of Torn from their Essex camp back to Derby. The numerous raiding parties which had been constantly upon the road during the days they had spent in this rich district had loaded the extra sumpter beasts with rich and valuable booty and the men, for the time satiated with fighting and loot, turned their faces toward Torn with evident satisfaction.

The outlaw was speaking to his captains in council; at his side the old man of Torn.

"Ride by easy stages, Shandy, and I will overtake you by tomorrow morning. I but ride for a moment to the castle of De Tany on an errand, and as I shall stop there but a few moments I shall surely join you tomorrow."

"Do not forget, My Lord," said Edwild the Serf, a great yellow-haired Saxon giant, "that there be a party of the King's troops camped close by the road which branches to Tany."

"I shall give them plenty of room," replied Norman of Torn. "My neck itcheth not to be stretched," and he laughed and mounted.

Five minutes after he had cantered down the road from camp, Spizo the Spaniard, sneaking his horse unseen into the surrounding forest, mounted and spurred rapidly after him. The camp, in the throes of packing refractory, half broken sumpter animals, and saddling their own wild mounts, did not notice his departure. Only the little grim, gray, old man knew that he had gone, or why, or whither.

That afternoon as Roger de Condé was admitted to the castle of Richard de Tany, and escorted to a little room where he awaited the coming of the Lady Joan, a swarthy messenger handed a letter to the captain of the King's soldiers camped a few miles south of Tany.

The officer tore open the seal as the messenger turned and spurred back in the direction from which he had come.

And this was what he read:

Norman of Torn is now at the castle of Tany, without escort.

Instantly the call "to arms" and "mount" sounded through the camp; and in five minutes a hundred mercenaries galloped rapidly toward the castle of Richard de Tany, in the visions of their captain a great reward and honor and preferment for the capture of the mighty outlaw who was now almost within his clutches.

Three roads meet at Tany; one from the south along which the King's soldiers were now riding; one from the west which had guided Norman of Torn from his camp to the castle; and a third which ran northwest through Cambridge and Huntingdon toward Derby.

All unconscious of the rapidly approaching foes Norman of Torn waited composedly in the anteroom for Joan de Tany.

Presently she entered, clothed in the clinging house

garment of the period; a beautiful vision, made more beautiful by the suppressed excitement which caused the blood to surge beneath the velvet of her cheek, and her breasts to rise and fall above her fast beating heart.

She let him take her fingers in his and raise them to his lips, and then they stood looking into each other's eyes in silence for a long moment.

"I do not know how to tell you what I have come to tell," he said sadly. "I have not meant to deceive you to your harm, but the temptation to be with you and those whom you typify must be my excuse. I—" He paused. It was easy to tell her that he was the Outlaw of Torn, but if she loved him, as he feared, how was he to tell her that he loved only Bertrade de Montfort?

"You need tell me nothing," interrupted Joan de Tany. "I have guessed what you would tell me, Norman of Torn. 'The spell of moonlight and adventure is no longer upon us'—those are your own words, and still I am glad to call you friend."

The little emphasis she put upon the last word bespoke the finality of her decision that the Outlaw of Torn could be no more than friend to her.

"It is best," he replied, relieved that, as he thought, she felt no love for him now that she knew him for what he really was. "Nothing good could come to such as you, Joan, if the Devil of Torn could claim more of you than friendship; and so I think that for your peace of mind and for my own we will let it be as though you had never known me. I thank you that you have not been angry with me. Remember me only to think that in the hills of Derby a sword is at your service, without reward and without price. Should you ever need it, Joan, tell me that you will send for me—wilt promise me that, Joan?"

"I promise, Norman of Torn."

"Farewell," he said, and as he again kissed her hand he bent his knee to the ground in reverence. Then he rose to go, pressing a little packet into her palm. Their eyes met, and the man saw in that brief instant deep in the azure depths of the girl's that which tumbled the structure of his new-found complacency about his ears.

As he rode out into the bright sunlight upon the road which led northwest toward Derby, Norman of Torn bowed his head in sorrow, for he realized two things. One was that the girl he had left still loved him, and that some day, mayhap tomorrow, she would suffer because she had sent him away; and the other was that he did not love her, that his heart was locked in the fair breast of Bertrade de Montfort.

He felt himself a beast that he had allowed his loneliness and the aching sorrow of his starved, empty heart to lead him into this girl's life. That he had been new to women and newer still to love did not permit him to excuse himself, and a hundred times he cursed his folly and stupidity, and what he thought was fickleness.

But the unhappy affair had taught him one thing for certain: to know without question what love was, and that the memory of Bertrade de Montfort's lips would always be more to him than all the allurements possessed by the balance of the women of the world, no matter how charming, or how beautiful.

Another thing, a painful thing he had learned from it, too, that the attitude of Joan de Tany, daughter of an old and noble house, was but the attitude which the Outlaw of Torn must expect from any good woman of her class; what he must expect from Bertrade de Montfort when she learned that Roger de Condé was Norman of Torn.

The outlaw had scarce passed out of sight upon the road to Derby ere the girl, who still stood in an embrasure of the south tower, gazing with strangely drawn, sad face up the road which had swallowed him, saw a body of soldiers galloping rapidly toward Tany from the south.

The King's banner waved above their heads, and intuitively Joan de Tany knew for whom they sought at her father's castle. Quickly she hastened to the outer barbican that it might be she who answered their hail rather than one of the men-at-arms on watch there.

She had scarcely reached the ramparts of the outer gate ere the King's men drew rein before the castle.

In reply to their hail Joan de Tany asked their mission.

"We seek the outlaw, Norman of Torn, who hides now within this castle," replied the officer.

"There be no outlaw here," replied the girl, "but, if you wish, you may enter with half a dozen men and search the castle."

This the officer did and when he had assured himself that Norman of Torn was not within an hour had passed, and Joan de Tany felt certain that the Outlaw of Torn was too far ahead to be caught by the King's men; so she said:

"There was one here just before you came who called himself though by another name than Norman of Torn, possibly it is he ye seek."

"Which way rode he?" cried the officer.

"Straight toward the west by the middle road," lied Joan de Tany. And as the officer hurried from the castle and, with his men at his back, galloped furiously away toward the west, the girl sank down upon a bench, pressing her little hands to her throbbing temples.

Then she opened the packet which Norman of Torn had handed her, and within found two others. In one of these was a beautiful jeweled locket, and on the outside were the initials *JT*, and on the inside the initials *NT;* in the other was a golden hair ornament set with precious stones, and about it was wound a strand of her own silken tresses.

She looked long at the little trinkets and then, pressing them against her lips, she threw herself face down upon an oaken bench, her lithe young form racked with sobs.

She was indeed but a little girl, chained by the inexorable bonds of caste to a false ideal. Birth and station spelled honor to her, and honor, to the daughter of an English noble, was a mightier force even than love.

That Norman of Torn was an outlaw she might have forgiven, but that he was, according to report, a low fellow of no birth placed an impassable barrier between them.

For hours the girl lay sobbing upon the bench, whilst

within her raged the mighty battle of the heart against the head.

Thus her mother found her, and kneeling beside her, and with her arms about the girl's neck, tried to soothe her and to learn the cause of her sorrow. Finally it came, poured from the flood gates of a sorrowing heart; that wave of bitter misery and hopelessness which not even a mother's love could check.

"Joan, my dear daughter," cried Lady de Tany, "I sorrow with thee that thy love has been cast upon so bleak and impossible a shore. But it be better that thou hast learnt the truth ere it were too late; for, take my word upon it, Joan, the bitter humiliation such an alliance must needs have brought upon thee and thy father's house would soon have cooled thy love; nor could his have survived the sneers and affronts even the menials would have put upon him."

"Oh, mother, but I love him so," moaned the girl. "I did not know how much until he had gone, and the King's officer had come to search for him, and then the thought that all the power of a great throne and the mightiest houses of an entire kingdom were turned in hatred against him raised the hot blood of anger within me and the knowledge of my love surged through all my being. Mother, thou canst not know the honor, and the bravery, and the chivalry of the man as I do. Not since Arthur of Silures kept his round table hath ridden forth upon English soil so true a knight as Norman of Torn.

"Couldst thou but have seen him fight, my mother, and witnessed the honor of his treatment of thy daughter, and heard the tone of dignified respect in which he spoke of women thou wouldst have loved him, too, and felt that outlaw though he be, he is still more a gentleman than nine-tenths the nobles of England."

"But his birth, my daughter!" argued the Lady de Tany. "Some even say that the gall marks of his brass collar still showeth upon his neck, and others that he knoweth not himself the name of his own father, nor had he any mother."

Ah, but this was the mighty argument! Naught could the girl say to justify so heinous a crime as low birth. What a man did in those rough cruel days might be forgotten and forgiven but the sins of his mother or his grandfather in not being of noble blood, no matter howsoever wickedly attained, he might never overcome or live down.

Torn by conflicting emotions the poor girl dragged herself to her own apartment and there upon a restless, sleepless couch, beset by wild, impossible hopes, and vain, torturing regrets, she fought out the long, bitter night; until toward morning she solved the problem of her misery in the only way that seemed possible to her poor, tired, bleeding, little heart. When the rising sun shone through the narrow window it found Joan de Tany at peace with all about her; the carved golden hilt of the toy that had hung at her girdle protruded from her breast, and a thin line of crimson ran across the snowy skin to a little pool upon the sheet beneath her.

And so the cruel hand of a mighty revenge had reached out to crush another innocent victim.

CHAPTER XV

WHEN word of the death of Joan de Tany reached Torn no man could tell from outward appearance the depth of the suffering which the sad intelligence wrought on the master of Torn.

All that they who followed him knew was that certain unusual orders were issued, and that that same night the ten companies rode south toward Essex without other halt than for necessary food and water for man and beast.

When the body of Joan de Tany rode forth from her father's castle to the church at Colchester, and again as it was brought back to its final resting place in the castle's crypt, a thousand strange and silent knights, black draped, upon horses trapped in black, rode slowly behind the bier.

Silently they had come in the night preceding the funeral, and as silently they slipped away northward into the falling shadows of the following night.

No word had passed between those of the castle and the great troop of sable-clad warriors, but all within knew that the mighty Outlaw of Torn had come to pay homage to the memory of the daughter of De Tany, and all but the grieving mother wondered at the strangeness of the act.

As the horde of Torn approached their Derby stronghold their young leader turned the command over to Red Shandy and dismounted at the door of Father Claude's cottage.

"I am tired, Father," said the outlaw as he threw himself upon his accustomed bench. "Naught but sorrow and death follow in my footsteps. I and all my acts be accurst, and upon those I love the blight falleth."

"Alter thy ways, my son; follow my advice ere it be too late. Seek out a new and better life in another country and carve thy future into the semblance of glory and honor."

"Would that I might, my friend," answered Norman of Torn. "But hast thou thought on the consequences which surely would follow should I thus remove both heart and head from the thing that I have built?

"What suppose thou would result were Norman of Torn to turn his great band of cut-throats, leaderless, upon England? Hast thought on't, Father?

"Wouldst thou draw a single breath in security if thou knew Edwild the Serf were ranging unchecked through Derby? Edwild, those father was torn limb from limb upon the rack because he would not confess to killing a buck in the new forest, a buck which fell before the arrow of another man; Edwild, whose mother was burned for witchcraft by Holy Church.

"And Horsan the Dane, Father. How thinkest thou the safety of the roads would be for either rich or poor an I turned Horsan the Dane loose upon ye?

"And Pensilo the Spanish Don! A great captain, but a man absolutely without bowels of compassion. When first he joined us and saw our mark upon the foreheads of our dead, wishing to out-Herod Herod, he marked the living which fell into his hands with a red hot iron, branding a great P upon each cheek and burning out the right eye completely. Wouldst like to feel, Father, that Don Piedro Castro y Pensilo ranged free through forest and hill of England?

"And Red Shandy, and the two Florys, and Peter the Hermit, and One Eye Kanty, and Gropello, and Campanee, and Cobarth, and Mandecote, and the thousand others, each with a special hatred for some particular class or individual, and all filled with the lust of blood and rapine and loot.

"No, Father, I may not go yet, for the England I have been taught to hate I have learned to love, and I have it not in my heart to turn loose upon her fair breast the beasts of hell who know no law or order or decency other than that which I enforce."

As Norman of Torn ceased speaking the priest sat silent for many minutes.

"Thou hast indeed a grave responsibility, my son," he said at last. "Thou canst not well go unless thou takest thy horde with thee out of England, but even that may be possible; who knows other than God?"

"For my part," laughed the outlaw, "I be willing to leave it in His hands; which seems to be the way with Christians. When one would shirk a responsibility, or explain an error, lo, one shoulders it upon the Lord."

"I fear, my son," said the priest, "that what seed of reverence I have attempted to plant within thy breast hath borne poor fruit."

"That dependeth upon the viewpoint, Father; as I take not the Lord into partnership in my successes it seemeth to me to be but of a mean and poor spirit to saddle my sorrows and perplexities upon Him. I may be wrong, for I am ill-versed in religious matters, but my conception of God and scapegoat be not that they are synonymous."

"Religion, my son, be a bootless subject for argument between friends," replied the priest, "and further, there be that nearer my heart just now which I would ask thee. I may offend, but thou know I do not mean to. The question I would ask, is, dost wholly trust the old man whom thou call father?"

"I know of no treachery," replied the outlaw, "which he hath ever conceived against me. Why?"

"I ask because I have written to Simon de Montfort asking him to meet me and two others here upon an important matter. I have learned that he expects to be at his Leicester castle, for a few days, within the week. He is to notify me when he will come and I shall then send for thee and the old man of Torn; but it were as well, my son, that thou do not mention this matter to thy father, nor let him know when thou come hither to the meeting that De Montfort is to be present."

"As you say, Father," replied Norman of Torn. "I do not make head nor tail of thy wondrous intrigues, but that thou wish it done thus or so is sufficient. I must be off to Torn now, so I bid thee farewell."

Until the following spring Norman of Torn continued to occupy himself with occasional pillages against the royalists of the surrounding counties, and his patrols so covered the public highways that it became a matter of grievous import to the King's party, for no one was safe in the district who even so much as sympathized with the King's cause, and many were the dead foreheads that bore the grim mark of the Devil of Torn.

Though he had never formally espoused the cause of the barons, it now seemed a matter of little doubt but that, in any crisis, his grisly banner would be found on their side.

The long winter evenings within the castle of Torn were often spent in rough, wild carousals in the great hall, where a thousand men might sit at table singing, fighting and drinking until the gray dawn stole in through the east windows, or Peter the Hermit, the fierce major-domo, tired of the din and racket came stalking into the chamber with drawn sword and laid upon the revellers with the flat of it to enforce the authority of his commands to disperse.

Norman of Torn and the old man seldom joined in these wild orgies, but when minstrel, or troubadour, or storyteller wandered to his grim lair the Outlaw of Torn would sit enjoying the break in the winter's dull monotony to as late an hour as another; nor could any man of his great fierce horde outdrink their chief when he cared to indulge in the pleasures of the wine cup. The only effect that liquor seemed to have upon him was to increase his desire to fight, so that he was wont to pick needless quarrels and to resort to his sword for the slightest, or for no provocation at all. So, for this reason, he drank but seldom since he always regretted the things he did under the promptings of that other self which only could assert its ego when reason was threatened with submersion.

Often on these evenings the company was entertained by stories from the wild, roving lives of its own members. Tales of adventure, love, war and death in every known corner of the world; and the ten captains told, each, his story of how he came to be of Torn; and thus, with fighting enough by day to keep them good humored, the winter passed, and spring came with the ever wondrous miracle of awakening life, with soft zephyrs, warm rain, and sunny skies.

Through all the winter Father Claude had been expecting to hear from Simon de Montfort but not until now did he receive a message which told the good priest that his letter had missed the great baron and had followed him around until he had but just received it. The message closed with these words:

"Any clew however vague which might lead nearer to a true knowledge of the fate of Prince Richard we shall most gladly receive and give our best attention. Therefore if thou wilst find it convenient we shall visit thee, good father, on the fifth day from today."

Spizo the Spaniard had seen De Montfort's man leave the note with Father Claude and he had seen the priest hide it under a great bowl on his table, so that when the good father left his cottage it was the matter of but a moment's work for Spizo to transfer the message from its hiding place to the breast of his tunic. The fellow could not read, but he to whom he took the missive could, laboriously, decipher the Latin in which it was penned.

The old man of Torn fairly trembled with suppressed rage as the full purport of this letter flashed upon him. It had been years since he had heard aught of the search for the little lost prince of England, and now that the period of his silence was drawing to a close, now that more and more often opportunities were opening up to him to wreak the last shred of his terrible vengeance, the very thought of being thwarted at the final moment staggered his comprehension.

"On the fifth day," he repeated. "That is the day on which we were to ride south again. Well, we shall ride, and Simon de Montfort shall not talk with thee, thou fool priest."

That same spring evening in the year 1264 a messenger drew rein before the walls of Torn and, to the challenge of the watch, cried:

"A royal messenger from His Illustrious Majesty, Henry, by the grace of God, King of England, Lord of Ireland, Duke of Aquitaine, to Norman of Torn. Open, in the name of the King!"

Norman of Torn directed that the King's messenger be admitted, and the knight was quickly ushered into the great hall of the castle.

The outlaw presently entered in full armor, with visor lowered.

The bearing of the King's officer was haughty and arrogant, as became a man of birth when dealing with a low born knave.

"His Majesty has deigned to address you, sirrah,"

he said, withdrawing a parchment from his breast. "And as you doubtless cannot read I will read the King's commands to you."

"I can read," replied Norman of Torn, "whatever the King can write. Unless it be," he added, "that the King writes no better than he rules."

The messenger scowled angrily, crying:

"It ill becomes such a low fellow to speak thus disrespectfully of our gracious King. If he were less generous he would have sent you a halter rather than this message which I bear."

"A bridle for thy tongue, my friend," replied Norman of Torn, "were in better taste than a halter for my neck. But come, let us see what the King writes to his friend, the Outlaw of Torn."

Taking the parchment from the messenger, Norman of Torn read:

Henry, by Grace of God, King of England, Lord of Ireland, Duke of Aquitaine; to Norman of Torn:

Since it has been called to our notice that you be harassing and plundering the persons and property of our faithful lieges—

We therefore, by virtue of the authority vested in us by Almighty God do command that you cease these nefarious practices—

And further, through the gracious intercession of Her Majesty, Queen Eleanor, we do offer you full pardon for all your past crimes—

Provided, you repair at once to the town of Lewes, with all the fighting men, your followers, prepared to

protect the security of our person, and wage war upon
those enemies of England, Simon de Montfort, Gilbert
de Clare, and their accomplices, who even now are
collected to threaten and menace our person and king-
dom—

Or, otherwise, shall you suffer death, by hanging, for
your long unpunished crimes. Witnessed myself, at
Lewes, on May the third, in the forty-eighth year of
our reign.

HENRY, REX.

"The closing paragraph be unfortunately worded,"
said Norman of Torn, "for because of it shall the King's
messenger eat the King's message; and thus take
back in his belly the answer of Norman of Torn."
And crumpling the parchment in his hand, he advanced
toward the royal emissary.

The knight whipped out his sword, but the Devil of
Torn was even quicker, so that it seemed that the
King's messenger had deliberately hurled his weapon
across the room, so quickly did the outlaw disarm him.

And then Norman of Torn took the man by the neck
with one powerful hand, and, despite his struggles, and
the beating of his mailed fists, bent him back upon the
table, and there, forcing his teeth apart with the point
of his sword, Norman of Torn rammed the King's message down the knight's throat; wax, parchment and
all.

It was a crestfallen gentleman who rode forth from
the castle of Torn a half hour later and spurred rapidly

202

southward; in his stomach a King's message, and in his head a more civil tongue.

When, two days later, he appeared before the King at Winchelsea and reported the outcome of his mission Henry raged and stormed, swearing by all the saints in the calendar that Norman of Torn should hang for his effrontery before the snow flew again.

News of the fighting between the barons and the King's forces at Rochester, Battel and elsewhere reached the ears of Norman of Torn a few days after the coming of the King's message, but at the same time came other news which hastened his departure toward the south. This latter word was that Bertrade de Montfort and her mother, accompanied by Prince Philip, had landed at Dover, and that upon the same boat had come Peter of Colfax back to England. The latter doubtless reassured by the strong conviction, which held in the minds of all royalists at that time, of the certainty of victory for the royal arms in the impending conflict with the rebel barons.

Norman of Torn had determined that he would see Bertrade de Montfort once again, and clear his conscience by a frank avowal of his identity. He knew what the result must be; his experience with Joan de Tany had taught him that. But the fine sense of chivalry which ever dominated all his acts where the happiness or honor of women were concerned urged him to give himself over as a sacrifice upon the altar of a woman's pride, that it might be she who spurned and rejected; for, as it must appear now, it had been he whose love had grown cold. It was a bitter thing to contemplate, for not alone would the mighty pride of the man be lacerated, but a great love.

Two days before the start of the march Spizo the Spaniard reported to the old man of Torn that he had overheard Father Claude ask Norman of Torn to come with his father to the priest's cottage the morning of the march to meet Simon de Montfort upon an important matter, but what the nature of the thing was the priest did not reveal to the outlaw.

This report seemed to please the little, grim, gray old man more than aught he had heard in several days; for it made it apparent that the priest had not as yet divulged the tenor of his conjecture to the Outlaw of Torn.

On the evening of the day preceding that set for the march south, a little, wiry figure, grim and gray, entered the cottage of Father Claude. No man knows what words passed between the good priest and his visitor nor the details of what befell within the four walls of the little cottage that night; but some half hour only elapsed before the little, grim, gray man emerged from the darkened interior and hastened upward upon the rocky trail into the hills, a cold smile of satisfaction on his lips.

The castle of Torn was filled with the rush and rattle of preparation early the following morning, for by eight o'clock the column was to march. The courtyard was filled with hurrying squires and lackeys. War horses were being groomed and caparisoned; sumpter beasts, snubbed to great posts, were being laden with the tents, bedding, and belongings of the men; while those already packed were wandering loose among the other animals and men. There was squealing, biting, kicking, and cursing as animals fouled one another with their loads, or brushed against some tethered war horse.

Squires were running hither and thither, or aiding their masters to don armor, lacing helm to hauberk, tying the points of ailette, coude, and rondel; buckling cuisse and jambe to thigh and leg. The open forges of armorer and smithy smoked and hissed, and the din of hammer on anvil rose above the thousand lesser noises of the castle courts, the shouting of commands, the rattle of steel, the ringing of iron hoof on stone flags, as these artificers hastened, sweating and cursing, through the eleventh hour repairs to armor, lance and sword, or to reset a shoe upon a refractory, plunging beast.

Finally the captains came, armored cap-a-pie, and with them some semblance of order and quiet out of chaos and bedlam. First the sumpter beasts, all loaded now, were driven, with a strong escort, to the downs below the castle and there held to await the column. Then, one by one, the companies were formed and marched out beneath fluttering pennon and waving banner to the martial strains of bugle and trumpet.

Last of all came the catapults, those great engines of destruction which hurled two hundred pound bowlders with mighty force against the walls of beleaguered castles.

And after all had passed through the great gates Norman of Torn and the little old man walked side by side from the castle building and mounted their chargers held by two squires in the center of the court-yard.

Below, on the downs, the column was forming in marching order, and as the two rode out to join it the little old man turned to Norman of Torn, saying,

"I had almost forgot a message I have for you, my son. Father Claude sent word last evening that he had been called suddenly south, and that some appointment you had with him must therefore be deferred until later; he said that you would understand." The old man eyed his companion narrowly through the eye slit in his helm.

" 'Tis passing strange," said Norman of Torn but that was his only comment. And so they joined the column which moved slowly down toward the valley and as they passed the cottage of Father Claude, Norman of Torn saw that the door was closed and that there was no sign of life about the place. A wave of melancholy passed over him, for the deserted aspect of the little flower hedged cote seemed dismally prophetic of a near future without the beaming, jovial face of his friend and adviser.

Scarcely had the horde of Torn passed out of sight down the east edge of the valley ere a party of richly dressed knights, coming from the south by another road along the west bank of the river, crossed over and drew rein before the cottage of Father Claude.

As their hails were unanswered one of the party dismounted to enter the building.

"Have a care, My Lord," cried his companion. "This

be over close to the Castle Torn and there may easily be more treachery than truth in the message which called thee thither."

"Fear not," replied Simon de Montfort, "the Devil of Torn hath no quarrel with me." Striding up the little path he knocked loudly on the door. Receiving no reply he pushed it open and stepped into the dim light of the interior. There he found his host, the good father Claude, stretched upon his back on the floor, the breast of his priestly robes dark with dried and clotted blood.

Turning again to the door, De Montfort summoned a couple of his companions.

"The secret of the little lost prince of England be a dangerous burden for a man to carry," he said. "But this convinces me more than any words the priest might have uttered that the abductor be still in England, and possibly Prince Richard also."

A search of the cottage revealed the fact that it had been ransacked thoroughly by the assassin. The contents of drawer and box littered every room, though that the object was not rich plunder was evidenced by many pieces of jewelry and money which remained untouched.

"The true object lies here," said De Montfort, pointing to the open hearth upon which lay the charred remains of many papers and documents. "All written evidence has been destroyed, but hold what lieth here beneath the table?" and, stooping, the Earl of Leicester picked up a sheet of parchment on which a letter had been commenced. It was addressed to him, and he read it aloud:

Lest some unforeseen chance should prevent the accomplishment of our meeting, My Lord Earl, I send thee this by one who knoweth not either its contents or the suspicions which I will narrate herein.

He who bareth this letter I truly believe to be the lost Prince Richard. Question him closely, My Lord, and I know that thou wilt be as positive as I.

Of his past thou know nearly as much as I, though thou may not know the wondrous chivalry and true nobility of character of him men call—

Here the letter stopped, evidently cut short by the dagger of the assassin.

"*Mon Dieu!* The damnable luck!" cried De Montfort, "but a second more and the name we have sought for twenty years would have been writ. Didst ever see such hellish chance as plays into the hand of the fiend incarnate since that long gone day when his sword pierced the heart of Lady Maud by the postern gate beside the Thames? The Devil himself must watch o'er him.

"There be naught more we can do here," he continued. "I should have been on my way to Fletching hours since. Come, my gentlemen, we will ride south by way of Leicester and have the good Fathers there look to the decent burial of this holy man."

The party mounted and rode rapidly away. Noon

found them at Leicester, and three days later they rode into the baronial camp at Fletching.

At almost the same hour the monks of the Abbey of Leicester performed the last rites of Holy Church for the peace of the soul of Father Claude and consigned his clay to the churchyard.

And thus another innocent victim of an insatiable hate and vengeance which had been born in the King's armory twenty years before passed from the eyes of men.

CHAPTER XVI

WHILE Norman of Torn and his thousand fighting men marched slowly south on the road toward Dover, the army of Simon de Montfort was preparing for its advance upon Lewes, where King Henry, with his son Prince Edward, and his brother, Prince Richard, King of the Romans, together with the latter's son, were entrenched with their forces, sixty thousand strong.

Before sunrise on a May morning in the year 1264, the barons' army set out from its camp at Fletching, nine miles from Lewes, and, marching through dense forests, reached a point two miles from the city, unobserved.

From here they ascended the great ridge of the hills up the valley Combe, the projecting shoulder of the Downs covering their march from the town. The King's party, however, had no suspicion that an attack was imminent, and, in direct contrast to the methods of the baronial troops, had spent the preceding night in drunken revelry, so that they were quite taken by surprise.

It is true that Henry had stationed an outpost upon the summit of the hill in advance of Lewes, but so lax was discipline in his army that the soldiers, growing tired of the duty, had abandoned the post toward morning, and returned to town, leaving but a single man on watch. He, left alone, had promptly fallen asleep; and thus De Montfort's men found and captured him within sight of the bell-tower of the Priory of Lewes, where the King and his royal allies lay peacefully asleep, after their night of wine and dancing and song.

Had it not been for an incident which now befell, the baronial army would doubtless have reached the city without being detected, but it happened that the evening before Henry had ordered a foraging party to ride forth at daybreak, as provisions for both men and beasts were low.

This party had scarcely left the city behind them ere they fell into the hands of the baronial troops. Though some few were killed or captured those who escaped were sufficient to arouse the sleeping army of the royalists to the close proximity and gravity of their danger.

By this time the four divisions of De Montfort's army were in full view of the town. On the left were the Londoners under Nicholas de Segrave; in the center rode De Clare, with John Fitz-John and William de Monchensy, at the head of a large division which occupied that branch of the hill which descended a gentle, unbroken slope to the town. The right wing was commanded by Henry de Montfort, the oldest son of Simon de Montfort, and with him was the third son, Guy, as well as John de Burgh and Humphrey de Bohun. The reserves were under Simon de Montfort himself.

Thus was the flower of English chivalry pitted against the King and his party, which included many nobles whose kinsmen were with De Montfort; so that brother faced brother, and father fought against son, on that bloody Wednesday, before the old town of Lewes.

Prince Edward was the first of the royal party to take the field, and as he issued from the castle with his gallant company, banners and pennons streaming in the breeze and burnished armor and flashing blade scintillating in the morning sunlight, he made a gorgeous and impressive spectacle as he hurled himself upon the Londoners, whom he had selected for attack because of the affront they had put upon his mother that day at London on the preceding July.

So vicious was his onslaught that the poorly armed and unprotected burghers, unused to the stern game of war, fell like sheep before the iron men on their iron shod horses. The long lances, the heavy maces, the six-bladed battle axes, and the well tempered swords of the knights played havoc among them, so that the rout was complete; but, not content with victory, Prince Edward must glut his vengeance, and so he pursued the citizens for miles, butchering great numbers of them, while many more were drowned in attempting to escape across the Ouse.

The left wing of the royalist army, under the King of the Romans and his gallant son, was not so fortunate for they met a determined resistance at the hands of Henry de Montfort.

The central divisions of the two armies seemed well matched also, and thus the battle continued throughout the day, the greatest advantage appearing to lie with the King's troops. Had Edward not gone so far afield in pursuit of the Londoners, the victory might easily have been on the side of the royalists early in the day, but by thus eliminating his division after defeating a part of De Montfort's army, it was as though neither of these two forces had been engaged.

The wily Simon de Montfort had attempted a little ruse which centered the fighting for a time upon the crest of one of the hills. He had caused his car to be placed there, with the tents and luggage of many of his leaders, under a small guard, so that the banners there displayed, together with the car, led the King of the Romans to believe that the Earl himself lay there, for Simon de Montfort had but a month or so before suffered an injury to his hip, when his horse fell with him, and the royalists were not aware that he had recovered sufficiently to again mount a horse.

And so it was that the forces under the King of the Romans pushed back the men of Henry de Montfort, and ever and ever closer to the car came the royalists until they were able to fall upon it, crying out insults against the old Earl and commanding him to come forth. And when they had killed the occupants of the car they found that Simon de Montfort was not among them, but instead he had fastened there three important citizens of London, old men and influential, who had opposed him, and aided and abetted the King.

So great was the wrath of Prince Richard, King of the Romans, that he fell upon the baronial troops with renewed vigor, and slowly but steadily beat them back from the town.

This sight, together with the routing of the enemy's left wing by Prince Edward, so cheered and inspired the royalists that the two remaining divisions took up the attack with refreshed spirits so that what a moment before had hung in the balance now seemed an assured victory for King Henry.

Both De Montfort and the King had thrown themselves into the mêlée with all their reserves; no longer was there semblance of organization. Division was inextricably bemingled with division; friend and foe formed a jumbled confusion of fighting, cursing chaos, over which whipped the angry pennons and banners of England's noblest houses.

That the mass seemed moving ever away from Lewes indicated that the King's arms were winning toward victory, and so it might have been had not a new element been infused into the battle; for now upon the brow of the hill to the north of them appeared a great horde of armored knights, and as they came into position where they could view the battle the leader raised his sword on high, and, as one man, the thousand broke into a mad charge.

Both De Montfort and the King ceased fighting as they gazed upon this body of fresh, well armored, well mounted reinforcements. Whom might they be? To which side owned they allegiance? And, then, as the black falcon wing on the banners of the advancing horsemen became distinguishable, they saw that it was the Outlaw of Torn.

Now he was close upon them, and had there been any doubt before, the wild battle cry which rang from a thousand fierce throats turned the hopes of the royalists cold within their breasts.

"For De Montfort! For De Montfort!" and "Down with Henry!" rang loud and clear above the din of battle.

Instantly the tide turned, and it was by only the barest chance that the King himself escaped capture, and regained the temporary safety of Lewes.

The King of the Romans took refuge within an old mill, and here it was that Norman of Torn found him barricaded. When the door was broken down the outlaw entered and dragged the monarch forth with his own hand to the feet of De Montfort, and would have put him to death had not the Earl intervened.

"I have yet to see my mark upon the forehead of a King," said Norman of Torn, "and the temptation be great; but, an you ask it, My Lord Earl, his life shall be yours to do with as you see fit."

"You have fought well this day, Norman of Torn," replied De Montfort. "Verily do I believe we owe our victory to you alone; so do not mar the record of a noble deed by wanton acts of atrocity."

"It is but what they had done to me, were I the prisoner instead," retorted the outlaw.

And Simon de Montfort could not answer that, for it was but the simple truth.

"How comes it, Norman of Torn," asked De Montfort as they rode together toward Lewes, "that you threw the weight of your sword upon the side of the barons? Be it because you hate the King more?"

"I do not know that I hate either, My Lord Earl," replied the outlaw. "I have been taught since birth to hate you all, but why I should hate was never told me. Possibly it be but a bad habit that will yield to my maturer years.

"As for why I fought as I did today," he continued, "it be because the heart of Lady Bertrade your daughter be upon your side. Had it been with the King, her uncle, Norman of Torn had fought otherwise than he has this day. So you see, My Lord Earl, you owe me no gratitude. Tomorrow I may be pillaging your friends as of yore."

Simon de Montfort turned to look at him, but the blank wall of his lowered visor gave no sign of the thoughts that passed beneath.

"You do much for a mere friendship, Norman of Torn," said the Earl coldly, "and I doubt me not but that my daughter has already forgot you. An English noblewoman, preparing to become a princess of France, does not have much thought to waste upon highwaymen." His tone, as well as his words were studiously arrogant and insulting, for it had stung the pride of this haughty noble to think that a low-born knave boasted the friendship of his daughter.

Norman of Torn made no reply, and could the Earl of Leicester have seen his face he had been surprised to note that instead of grim hatred and resentment, the features of the Outlaw of Torn were drawn in lines of pain and sorrow; for he read in the attitude of the father what he might expect to receive at the hands of the daughter.

CHAPTER XVII

WHEN those of the royalists who had not deserted the King and fled precipitably toward the coast had regained the castle and the Priory the city was turned over to looting and rapine. In this Norman of Torn and his men did not participate, but camped a litle apart from the town until daybreak the following morning, when they started east, toward Dover.

They marched until late the following evening, passing some twenty miles out of their way to visit a certain royalist stronghold. The troops stationed there had fled, having been appraised some few hours earlier, by fugitives, of the defeat of Henry's army at Lewes.

Norman of Torn searched the castle for the one he sought, but, finding it entirely deserted, continued his eastward march. Some few miles farther on he overtook a party of deserting royalist soldiery, and from them he easily, by dint of threats, elicited the information he desired: the direction taken by the refugees from the deserted castle, their number, and as close a description of the party as the soldiers could give.

Again he was forced to change the direction of his march, this time heading northward into Kent. It was dark before he reached his destination, and saw before him the familiar outlines of the castle of Roger de Leybourn. This time the outlaw threw his fierce horde completely around the embattled pile, before he advanced with a score of sturdy ruffians to reconnoiter.

Making sure that the drawbridge was raised, and

that he could not hope for stealthy entrance there, he crept silently to the rear of the great building, and there among the bushes his men searched for the ladder that Norman of Torn had seen the knavish servant of My Lady Claudia unearth, that the outlaw might visit the Earl of Buckingham, unannounced.

Presently they found it, and it was the work of but a moment to raise it to the sill of the low window, so that soon the twenty stood beside their chief within the walls of Leybourn.

Noiselessly they moved through the halls and corridors of the castle until a maid, bearing a great pasty from the kitchen, turned a sudden corner and bumped full into the Outlaw of Torn. With a shriek that might have been heard at Lewes she dropped the dish upon the stone floor, and, turning, ran, still shrieking at the top of her lungs, straight for the great dining hall.

So close behind her came the little band of outlaws that scarce had the guests arisen in consternation from the table at the shrill cries of the girl than Norman of Torn burst through the great door with twenty drawn swords at his back.

The hall was filled with knights and gentlewomen and house servants and men-at-arms. Fifty swords flashed from fifty scabbards as the men of the party saw the hostile appearance of their visitors, but before a blow could be struck Norman of Torn, grasping his sword in his right hand, raised his left aloft in a gesture for silence.

"Hold!" he cried, and, turning directly to Roger de Leybourn, "I have no quarrel with thee, My Lord; but again I come for a guest within thy halls. Methinks thou hast as bad taste in whom thou entertains as didst thy fair lady."

"Who be ye, that thus rudely breaks in upon the peace of my castle, and makes bold to insult my guests?" demanded Roger de Leybourn.

"Who be I! If you wait you shall see my mark upon the forehead of yon grinning baboon," replied the outlaw, pointing a mailed finger at one who had been seated close to De Leybourn.

All eyes turned in the direction that the rigid finger of the outlaw indicated, and there indeed was a fearful apparition of a man. With livid face he stood, leaning for support against the table; his craven knees wabbling beneath his fat carcass; while his lips were drawn apart against his yellow teeth in a horrid grimace of awful fear.

"If you recognize me not, Sir Roger," said Norman of Torn, drily, "it is evident that your honored guest hath a better memory."

At last the fear struck man found his tongue, and, though his eyes never left the menacing figure of the grim, iron-clad outlaw, he addressed the master of Leybourn; shrieking in a high, awe emasculated falsetto:

"Seize him! Kill him! Set your men upon him! Do you wish to live another moment draw and defend yourselves for he be the Devil of Torn, and there be a great price upon his head.

"Oh, save me, save me! for he has come to kill me," he ended in a pitiful wail.

The Devil of Torn! How that name froze the hearts of the assembled guests.

The Devil of Torn! Slowly the men standing there at the board of Sir Roger de Leybourn grasped the full purport of that awful name.

Tense silence for a moment held the room in the stillness of a sepulchre, and then a woman shrieked, and fell prone across the table. She had seen the mark of the Devil of Torn upon the dead brow of her mate.

And then Roger de Leybourn spoke:

"Norman of Torn, but once before have you entered within the walls of Leybourn, and then you did, in the service of another, a great service for the house of Leybourn; and you stayed the night, an honored guest. But a moment since you said that you had no quarrel with me. Then why be you here? Speak! Shall it be as a friend or an enemy that the master of Leybourn greets Norman of Torn; shall it be with outstretched hand or naked sword?"

"I come for this man whom you may all see has good reason to fear me. And when I go I take part of him with me. I be in a great hurry, so I would prefer to take my great and good friend, Peter of Colfax, without interference; but, if you wish it otherwise; we be a score strong within your walls, and nigh a thousand lie without. What say you, My Lord?"

"Your grievance against Peter of Colfax must be a mighty one, that you search him out thus within a day's ride from the army of the King who has placed a price upon your head, and from another army of men who be equally your enemies."

"I would gladly go to hell after Peter of Colfax," replied the outlaw. "What my grievance be matters not. Norman of Torn acts first and explains afterward, if he cares to explain at all. Come forth, Peter of Colfax, and for once in your life, fight like a man, that you may save your friends here from the fate that has found you at last after two years of patient waiting."

Slowly the palsied limbs of the great coward bore him tottering to the center of the room, where gradually a little clear space had been made; the men of the party forming a circle, in the center of which stood Peter of Colfax and Norman of Torn.

"Give him a great draught of brandy," said the outlaw, "or he will sink down and choke in the froth of his own terror."

When they had forced a goblet of the fiery liquid upon him, Peter of Colfax regained his lost nerve enough so that he could raise his sword arm and defend himself; and as the fumes circulated through him, and the primal instinct of self-preservation asserted itself, he put up a more and more creditable fight, until those who watched thought that he might indeed have a chance to vanquish the Outlaw of Torn. But they did not know that Norman of Torn was but playing with his victim, that he might make the torture long drawn out, and wreak as terrible a punishment upon Peter of Colfax, before he killed him, as the Baron had visited upon Bertrade de Monfort because she would not yield to his base desires.

The guests were craning their necks to follow every detail of the fascinating drama that was being enacted before them.

"God, what a swordsman!" muttered one.

"Never was such sword play seen since the day the first sword was drawn from the first scabbard!" replied Roger de Leybourn. "Is it not marvellous!"

Slowly but surely was Norman of Torn cutting Peter of Colfax to pieces; little by little, and with such fiendish care that except for loss of blood, the man was in no way crippled; nor did the outlaw touch his victim's face with his gleaming sword; *that* he was saving for the fulfillment of his design.

And Peter of Colfax, cornered and fighting for his life, was no marrowless antagonist, even against the Devil of Torn. Furiously he fought; in the extremity of his fear rushing upon his executioner with frenzied agony. Great beads of cold sweat stood upon his livid brow.

And then the gleaming point of Norman of Torn flashed, lightning-like, in his victim's face, and above the right eye of Peter of Colfax was a thin vertical cut from which the red blood had barely started to ooze ere another swift move of that master sword hand placed a fellow to parallel the first.

Five times did the razor point touch the forehead of Peter of Colfax, until the watchers saw there, upon the brow of the doomed man, the seal of death, in letters of blood—NT.

It was the end. Peter of Colfax, cut to ribbons yet fighting like the maniac he had become, was as good as dead, for the mark of the Outlaw of Torn was upon his brow. Now, shrieking and gibbering through his frothy lips, his yellow fangs bared in a mad and horrid grin, he rushed full upon Norman of Torn. There was a flash of the great sword as the outlaw swung it to the full of his mighty strength through an arc that passed above the shoulders of Peter of Colfax, and the grinning head rolled upon the floor, while the loathsome carcass, that had been a baron of England, sunk in a disheveled heap among the rushes of the great hall of the castle of Leybourn.

A little shudder passed through the wide-eyed guests. Some one broke into hysterical laughter, a woman sobbed, and then Norman of Torn, wiping his blade upon the rushes of the floor as he had done upon another occasion in that same hall, spoke quietly to the master of Leybourn.

"I would borrow yon golden platter, My Lord. It shall be returned, or a mightier one in its stead."

Leybourn nodded his assent, and Norman of Torn turned, with a few words of instructions, to one of his men.

The fellow gathered up the head of Peter of Colfax, and placed it upon the golden platter.

"I thank you, Sir Roger, for your hospitality," said Norman of Torn, with a low bow which included the spellbound guests. "Adieu." Thus followed by his men, one bearing the head of Peter of Colfax upon the platter of gold, Norman of Torn passed quietly from the hall and from the castle.

CHAPTER XVIII

BOTH horses and men were fairly exhausted from the gruelling strain of many days of marching and fighting, so Norman of Torn went into camp that night; nor did he again take up his march until the second morning, three days after the battle of Lewes.

He bent his direction toward the north and Leicester's castle, where he had reason to believe he would find a certain young woman, and though it galled his sore heart to think upon the humiliation that lay waiting his coming, he could not do less than that which he felt his honor demanded.

Beside him on the march rode the fierce red giant, Shandy, and the wiry, gray little man of Torn, whom the outlaw called father.

In no way, save the gray hair and the parchment-surfaced skin, had the old fellow changed in all these years. Without bodily vices, and clinging ever to the open air and the exercise of the foil he was still young in muscle and endurance.

For five years he had not crossed foils with Norman of Torn, but he constantly practiced with the best swordsmen of the wild horde, so that it had become a subject often discussed among the men as to which of the two, father or son, was the greater swordsman.

Always taciturn, the old fellow rode in his usual silence. Long since had Norman of Torn usurped by the force of his strong character and masterful ways,

224

the position of authority in the castle of Torn. The old man simply rode and fought with the others when it pleased him; and he had come on this trip because he felt that there was that impending for which he had waited over twenty years.

Cold and hard, he looked with no love upon the man he still called "my son." If he held any sentiment toward Norman of Torn it was one of pride which began and ended in the almost fiendish skill of his pupil's mighty sword arm.

The little army had been marching for some hours when the advance guard halted a party bound south upon a crossroad. There were some twenty or thirty men, mostly servants, and a half dozen richly garbed knights.

As Norman of Torn drew rein beside them he saw that the leader of the party was a very handsome man of about his own age, and evidently a person of distinction; a profitable prize, thought the outlaw.

"Who are you," said the gentleman, in French, "that stops a prince of France upon the highroad as though he were an escaped criminal? Are you of the King's forces, or De Montfort's?"

"Be this Prince Philip of France?" asked Norman of Torn.

"Yes, but who be you?"

"And be you riding to meet my Lady Bertrade de Montfort?" continued the outlaw, ignoring the Prince's question.

"Yes, an it be any of your affair," replied Philip curtly.

"It be," said the Devil of Torn, "for I be a friend of My Lady Bertrade, and as the way be beset with dangers from disorganized bands of roving soldiery, it is unsafe for Monsieur le Prince to venture on with so small an escort. Therefore will the friend of Lady Bertrade de Montfort ride with Monsieur le Prince to his destination that Monsieur may arrive there safely."

"It is kind of you, Sir Knight, a kindness that I will not forget. But, again, who is it that shows this solicitude for Philip of France?"

"Norman of Torn, they call me," replied the outlaw.

"Indeed!" cried Philip. "The great and bloody outlaw?" Upon his handsome face there was no look of fear or repugnance.

Norman of Torn laughed.

"Monsieur le Prince thinks, mayhap, that he will make a bad name for himself," he said, "if he rides in such company?"

"My Lady Bertrade and her mother think you be less devil than saint," said the Prince. "They have told me of how you saved the daughter of De Montfort, and, ever since, I have been of a great desire to meet you, and to thank you. It had been my intention to ride to Torn for that purpose so soon as we reached Leicester, but the Earl changed all our plans by his victory; and only yesterday, on his orders the Princess Eleanor, his wife, with the Lady Bertrade, rode to Battel, where Simon de Montfort and the King are to be today. The Queen also is there with her retinue, so it be expected that, to show the good feeling and renewed friendship existing between De Montfort and his King, there will be gay scenes in the old fortress. But," he added, after a pause, "dare the Outlaw of Torn ride within reach of the King who has placed a price upon his head?"

"The price has been there since I was eighteen," answered Norman of Torn, "and yet my head be where it has always been. Can you blame me if I look with levity upon the King's price? It be not heavy enough to weigh me down; nor never has it held me from going where I listed in all England. I am freer than the King, My Lord, for the King be a prisoner today."

Together they rode toward Battel, and as they talked, Norman of Torn grew to like this brave and handsome gentleman. In his heart was no rancor because of the coming marriage of the man to the woman he loved. If Bertrade de Montfort loved this handsome French prince, then Norman of Torn was his friend; for his love was a great love, above jealousy. It not only held her happiness above his own, but the happiness and welfare of the man she loved, as well.

It was dusk when they reached Battel and as Norman of Torn bid the prince adieu, for the horde was to make camp just without the city, he said:

"May I ask My Lord to carry a message to Lady Bertrade? It is in reference to a promise I made her two years since and which I now, for the first time, be able to fulfill."

"Certainly, my friend," replied Philip. The outlaw, dismounting, called upon one of his squires for parchment, and, by the light of a torch, wrote a message to Bertrade de Montfort.

Half an hour later a servant in the castle of Battel handed the missive to the daughter of Leicester as she sat alone in her apartment. Opening it, she read:

To Lady Bertrade de Montfort, from her friend Norman of Torn.

Two years have passed since you took the hand of the Outlaw of Torn in friendship, and now he comes to sue for another favor.

It is that he may have speech with you, alone, in the castle of Battel this night.

Though the name Norman of Torn be fraught with terror to others, I know that you do not fear him, for you must know the loyalty and friendship which he bears you.

My camp lies without the city's gates, and your messenger will have safe conduct whatever reply he bears to,

Norman of Torn.

Fear? Fear Norman of Torn? The girl smiled as she thought of that moment of terrible terror two years ago when she learned, in the castle of Peter of Colfax, that she was alone with, and in the power of, the Devil of Torn. And then she recalled his little acts of thoughtful chivalry, nay, almost tenderness, on the long night ride to Leicester.

What a strange contradiction of a man! She wondered if he would come with lowered visor, for she was still curious to see the face that lay behind the cold, steel mask. She would ask him this night to let her see his face; or would that be cruel? For did they not say that it was from the very ugliness of it that he kept his helm closed to hide the repulsive sight from the eyes of men!

As her thoughts wandered back to her brief meeting with him two years before, she wrote and dispatched her reply to Norman of Torn.

In the great hall that night as the King's party sat at supper, Philip of France, addressing Henry, said:

"And who thinkest thou, My Lord King, rode by my side to Battel today, that I might not be set upon by knaves upon the highway?"

"Some of our good friends from Kent?" asked the King.

"Nay, it was a man upon whose head Your Majesty has placed a price, Norman of Torn; and if all of your English highwaymen be as courteous and pleasant gentlemen as he, I shall ride always alone and unarmed through your realm that I may add to my list of pleasant acquaintances."

"The Devil of Torn?" asked Henry, incredulously. "Some one be hoaxing you."

"Nay, Your Majesty, I think not," replied Philip, "for he was indeed a grim and mighty man, and at his back rode as ferocious and awe-inspiring a pack as ever I beheld outside a prison; fully a thousand strong they rode. They be camped not far without the city now."

"My Lord," said Henry, turning to Simon de Montfort, "be it not time that England were rid of this devil's spawn and his hellish brood? Though I presume," he added, a sarcastic sneer upon his lip, "that it may prove embarrassing for My Lord Earl of Leicester to turn upon his companion in arms."

"I owe him nothing," returned the Earl haughtily, "by his own word."

"You owe him victory at Lewes," snapped the King. "It were indeed a sad commentary upon the sincerity of our loyalty professing lieges who turned their arms against our royal person, 'to save him from the treachery of his false advisers,' that they called upon a cut-throat outlaw with a price upon his head to aid them in their 'righteous cause'."

"My Lord King," cried De Montfort, flushing with anger, "I called not upon this fellow, nor did I know he was within two hundred miles of Lewes until I saw him ride into the midst of the conflict that day. Neither did I know, until I heard his battle cry, whether he would fall upon baron or royalist."

"If that be the truth, Leicester," said the King, with a note of skepticism which he made studiously apparent, "hang the dog. He be just without the city even now."

"You be King of England, My Lord Henry. If you say that he shall be hanged, hanged he shall be," replied De Montfort.

"A dozen courts have already passed sentence upon him, it only remains to catch him, Leicester," said the King.

"A party shall sally forth at dawn to do the work," replied De Montforth.

"And not," thought Philip of France, "if I know it,

shall the brave Outlaw of Torn be hanged tomorrow."

In his camp without the city of Battel, Norman of Torn paced back and forth waiting an answer to his message.

Sentries patrolled the entire circumference of the bivouac, for the outlaw knew full well that he had put his head within the lion's jaw when he had ridden thus boldly to the seat of English power. He had no faith in the gratitude of De Montfort, and he knew full well what the King would urge when he learned that the man who had sent his soldiers naked back to London, who had forced his messenger to eat the King's message, and who had turned his victory to defeat at Lewes, was within reach of the army of De Montfort.

Norman of Torn loved to fight, but he was no fool, and so he did not relish pitting his thousand upon an open plain against twenty thousand within a walled fortress.

No, he would see Bertrade de Montfort that night and before dawn his rough band would be far on the road toward Torn. The risk was great to enter the castle, filled as it was with his mighty enemies. But if he died there it would be in a good cause, thought he; and, anyway, he had set himself to do this duty which he dreaded so, and do it he would were all the armies of the world camped within Battel.

Directly he heard a low challenge from one of his sentries, who presently appeared escorting a lackey.

"A messenger from Lady Bertrade de Montfort," said the soldier.

"Bring him hither," commanded the outlaw.

The lackey approached and handed Norman of Torn a dainty parchment sealed with scented wax wafers.

"Did My Lady say you were to wait for an answer?" asked the outlaw.

"I am to wait, My Lord," replied the awestruck fellow, to whom the service had been much the same had his mistress ordered him to Hell to bear a message to the Devil.

Norman of Torn turned to a flickering torch and, breaking the seals, read the message from the woman he loved. It was short and simple.

To Norman of Torn, from his friend always, Bertrade de Montfort.

Come with Giles. He has my instructions to lead thee secretly to where I be.

Bertrade de Montfort.

Norman of Torn turned to where one of his captains squatted upon the ground beside an object covered with a cloth.

"Come, Flory," he said, and then, turning to the waiting Giles, "lead on."

They fell in single file: first the lackey, Giles, then Norman of Torn and last the fellow whom he had addressed as Flory bearing the object covered with a cloth. But it was not Flory who brought up the rear. Flory lay dead in the shadow of a great oak within the camp; a thin wound below his left shoulder blade marked the spot where a keen dagger had found its way to his heart, and in his place walked the little grim, gray, old man, bearing the object covered with a cloth. But none might know the difference, for the little man wore the armor of Flory, and his visor was drawn.

And so they came to a small gate which let into the castle wall where the shadow of a great tower made the blackness of a black night doubly black. Through many dim corridors the lackey led them, and up winding stairways until presently he stopped before a low door.

"Here," he said, "My Lord," and turning left them.

Norman of Torn touched the panel with the mailed knuckles of his right hand, and a low voice from within whispered, "Enter."

Silently he strode into the apartment, a small ante-chamber off a large hall. At one end was an open hearth upon which logs were burning brightly, while a single lamp aided in diffusing a soft glow about the austere chamber. In the center of the room was a table, and at the sides several benches.

Before the fire stood Bertrade de Montfort, and she was alone.

"Place your burden upon this table, Flory," said Norman of Torn. And when it had been done: "You may go. Return to camp."

He did not address Bertrade de Montfort until the door had closed behind the little grim, gray man who wore the armor of the dead Flory and then Norman of Torn advanced to the table and stood with his left hand ungauntleted, resting upon the table's edge.

"My Lady Bertrade," he said at last, "I have come to fulfill a promise."

He spoke in French, and she started slightly at his voice. Before, Norman of Torn had always spoken in English. Where had she heard that voice! There were tones in it that haunted her.

"What promise did Norman of Torn e'er make to Bertrade de Montfort?" she asked. "I do not understand you, my friend."

"Look," he said. And as she approached the table he withdrew the cloth which covered the object that the man had placed there.

The girl started back with a little cry of terror, for there upon a golden platter was a man's head; horrid with the grin of death baring yellow fangs.

"Dost recognize the thing?" asked the outlaw. And then she did; but still she could not comprehend. At last, slowly, there came back to her the idle, jesting promise of Roger de Condé to fetch the head of her enemy to the feet of his princess, upon a golden dish.

But what had the Outlaw of Torn to do with that! It was all a sore puzzle to her, and then she saw the bared left hand of the grim, visored figure of the Devil of Torn, where it rested upon the table beside the grisly head of Peter of Colfax; and upon the third finger was the great ring she had tossed to Roger de Condé on that day, two years before.

What strange freak was her brain playing her! It could not be, no it was impossible; then her glance fell again upon the head grinning there upon the platter of gold, and upon the forehead of it she saw in letters of dried blood that awful symbol of sudden death—NT!

Slowly her eyes returned to the ring upon the out-

234

law's hand, and then up to his visored helm. A step she took toward him, one hand upon her breast, the other stretched pointing toward his face, and she swayed slightly as might one who has just arisen from a great illness.

"Your visor," she whispered, "raise your visor." And then, as though to herself: "It cannot be; it cannot be."

Norman of Torn, though it tore the heart from him, did as she bid, and there before her she saw the brave strong face of Roger de Condé.

"*Mon Dieu!*" she cried, "Tell me it is but a cruel joke."

"It be the cruel truth, My Lady Bertrade," said Norman of Torn sadly. And, then, as she turned away from him, burying her face in her raised arms, he came to her side, and, laying his hand upon her shoulder, said sadly:

"And now you see, My Lady, why I did not follow you to France. My heart went there with you, but I knew that naught but sorrow and humiliation could come to one whom the Devil of Torn loved, if that love was returned; and so I waited until you might forget the words you had spoken to Roger de Condé before I came to fulfill the promise that you should know him in his true colors.

"It is because I love you, Bertrade, that I have come this night. God knows that it be no pleasant thing to see the loathing in your very attitude, and to read the hate and revulsion that surges through your heart, or to guess the hard, cold thoughts which fill your mind against me because I allowed you to speak the words you once spoke, and to the Devil of Torn.

"I make no excuse for my weakness. I ask no forgiveness for what I know you never can forgive. That, when you think of me, it will always be with loathing and contempt is the best that I can hope.

"I only know that I love you, Bertrade; I only know that I love you, and with a love that surpasseth even my own understanding.

"Here is the ring that you gave in token of friendship. Take it. The hand that wore it has done no wrong by the light that has been given it as guide.

"The blood that has pulsed through the finger that it circled came from a heart that beat for Bertrade de Montfort; a heart that shall continue to beat for her alone until a merciful providence sees fit to gather in a wasted and useless life.

"Farewell, Bertrade." Kneeling he raised the hem of her garment to his lips.

A thousand conflicting emotions surged through the heart of this proud daughter of the new conqueror of England. The anger of an outraged confidence, gratitude for the chivalry which twice had saved her honor, hatred for the murderer of a hundred friends and kinsmen, respect and honor for the marvellous courage of the man, loathing and contempt for the base born, the memory of that exalted moment when those handsome lips had clung to hers, pride in the fearlessness of a champion who dared come alone among twenty thousand enemies for the sake of a promise made her; but stronger than all the rest two stood out before her mind's eye like living things—the degradation of his low birth, and the memory of the great love she had cherished all these long and dreary months.

And these two fought out their battle in the girl's breast. In those few brief moments of bewilderment and indecision it seemed to Bertrade de Montfort that ten years passed above her head, and when she reached her final resolution she was no longer a young girl but a grown woman who, with the weight of a mature deliberation, had chosen the path which she would travel to the end—to the final goal, however sweet or however bitter.

Slowly she turned toward him who knelt with bowed head at her feet, and, taking the hand that held the ring outstretched toward her, raised him to his feet. In silence she replaced the golden band upon his finger, and then she lifted her eyes to his.

"Keep the ring, Norman of Torn," she said. "The friendship of Bertrade de Montfort is not lightly given nor lightly taken away," she hesitated, "nor is her love."

"What do you mean?" he whispered. For in her eyes was that wondrous light he had seen there on that other day in the far castle of Leicester.

"I mean," she answered, "that, Roger de Condé or Norman of Torn, gentleman or highwayman, it be all the same to Bertrade de Montfort—it be thee I love; thee!"

Had she reviled him, spat upon him, he would not have been surprised, for he had expected the worst; but that she should love him! Oh God, had his over wrought nerves turned his poor head? Was he dreaming this thing, only to awaken to the cold and awful truth!

But these warm arms about his neck, the sweet perfume of the breath that fanned his cheek; these were no dream!

"Think thee what thou art saying, Bertrade?" he cried. "Dost forget that I be a low born knave, knowing not my own mother and questioning even the identity of my father? Could a De Montfort face the world with such a man for husband?"

"I know what I say, perfectly," she answered. "Were thou born out of wedlock, the son of a hostler and a scullery maid, still would I love thee, and honor thee, and cleave to thee. Where thou be, Norman of Torn, there shall be happiness for me. Thy friends shall be my friends; thy joys shall be my joys; thy sorrows, my sorrows; and thy enemies, even mine own father, shall be my enemies.

"Why it is, my Norman, I know not. Only do I know that I didst often question my own self if in truth I did really love Roger de Condé, but thee—oh Norman, why is it that there be no shred of doubt now, that this heart, this soul, this body be all and always for the Outlaw of Torn?"

"I do not know," he said simply and gravely. "So wonderful a thing be beyond my poor brain; but I think my heart knows, for in very joy it is sending the hot blood racing and surging through my being till I were like to be consumed for the very heat of my happiness."

"Sh!" she whispered, suddenly, "methinks I hear footsteps. They must not find thee here, Norman of Torn, for the King has only this night wrung a promise from my father to take thee in the morning and hang thee. What shall we do, Norman? Where shall we meet again?"

"We shall not be separated, Bertrade; only so long as it may take thee to gather a few trinkets, and fetch thy riding cloak. Thou ridest north tonight with Norman of Torn, and by the third day Father Claude shall make us one."

"I am glad thee wish it," she replied. "I feared that, for some reason, thee might not think it best for me to go with thee now. Wait here, I will be gone but a moment. If the footsteps I hear approach this door," and she indicated the door by which he had entered the little room, "thou canst step through this other doorway into the adjoining apartment, and conceal thyself there until the danger passes."

Norman of Torn made a wry face, for he had no stomach for hiding himself away from danger.

"For my sake," she pleaded. So he promised to do as she bid, and she ran swiftly from the room to fetch her belongings.

CHAPTER XIX

WHEN the little, grim, gray man had set the object covered with a cloth upon the table in the center of the room and left the apartment, he did not return to camp as Norman of Torn had ordered.

Instead he halted immediately without the little door, which he left a trifle ajar, and there he waited, listening to all that passed between Bertrade de Montfort and Norman of Torn.

As he heard the proud daughter of Simon de Montfort declare her love for the Devil of Torn a cruel smile curled his lip.

"It will be better than I had hoped," he muttered, "and easier. 'S blood! How much easier now that Leicester too may have his whole proud heart in the hanging of Norman of Torn. Ah, what a sublime revenge! I have waited long, thou cur of a King, to return the blow thou struck that day, but the return shall be an hundred fold increased by long accumulated interest."

Quickly the wiry figure hastened through the passageways and corridors, until he came to the great hall where sat De Montfort and the King, with Philip of France and many others, gentlemen and nobles.

Before the guard at the door could halt him he had broken into the room, and, addressing the King, cried:

"Wouldst take the Devil of Torn, My Lord King? He be now alone where a few men may seize him."

"What now! What now!" ejaculated Henry. "What madman be this?"

"I be no madman, Your Majesty; never did brain work more clearly or to more certain ends," replied the man.

"It may doubtless be some ruse of the cut-throat himself," cried De Montfort.

"Where be the knave?" asked Henry.

"He stands now within this palace and in his arms be Bertrade, daughter of My Lord Earl of Leicester. Even now she did but tell him that she loved him."

"Hold," cried De Montfort. "Hold fast thy foul tongue. What meanest thou by uttering such lies, and to my very face?"

"They be no lies, Simon de Montfort. An I tell thee that Roger de Condé and Norman of Torn be one and the same thou wilt know that I speak no lie."

De Montfort paled.

"Where be the craven wretch?" he demanded.

"Come," said the little, old man. And turning he led from the hall, closely followed by De Montfort, the King, Prince Philip and the others.

"Thou hadst better bring twenty fighting men—thou'lt need them all to take Norman of Torn," he advised De Montfort. And so as they passed the guard room the party was increased by twenty men-at-arms.

Scarcely had Bertrade de Montfort left him ere Norman of Torn heard the tramping of many feet. They seemed approaching up the dim corridor that led to the little door of the apartment where he stood.

Quickly he moved to the opposite door, and, standing with his hand upon the latch, waited. Yes, they were coming that way, many of them and quickly; and as he heard them pause without he drew aside the arras and pushed open the door behind him; backing into the other apartment just as Simon de Montfort, Earl of Leicester, burst into the room from the opposite side.

At the same instant a scream rang out behind Norman of Torn, and, turning, he faced a brightly lighted room in which sat Eleanor, Queen of England, and another Eleanor, wife of Simon de Montfort, with their ladies.

There was no hiding now, and no escape; for run he would not, even had there been where to run. Slowly he backed away from the door toward a corner, where with his back against a wall and a table at his right, he might die as he had lived, fighting; for Norman of Torn knew that he could hope for no quarter from the men who had him cornered there like a great bear in a trap.

With an army at their call it were an easy thing to take a lone man, even though that man were the Devil of Torn.

The King and De Montfort had now crossed the smaller apartment and were within the room where the outlaw stood at bay.

At the far side the group of royal and noble women stood huddled together, while behind De Montfort and the King pushed twenty gentlemen and as many men-at-arms.

"What dost thou here, Norman of Torn?" cried De Montfort, angrily. "Where be my daughter, Bertrade?"

"I be here, My Lord Earl, to attend to mine own

affairs," replied Norman of Torn, "which be the affair of no other man. As to your daughter: I know nothing of her whereabouts. What should she have to do with the Devil of Torn, My Lord?"

De Montfort turned toward the little gray man.

"He lies," shouted he. "Her kisses be yet wet upon his lips."

Norman of Torn looked at the speaker, and beneath the visor that was now partly raised he saw the features of the man whom, for twenty years, he had called father.

He had never expected love from this hard old man, but treachery and harm from him—no, he could not believe it, one of them must have gone mad; but why Flory's armor, where was the faithful Flory?

"Father!" he ejaculated, "leadest thou the hated English King against thine own son?"

"Thou be no son of mine, Norman of Torn," retorted the old man. "Thy days of usefulness to me be past; tonight thou serve me best swinging from a wooden gibbet. Take him, My Lord Earl; they say there be a good strong gibbet in the courtyard below."

"Wilt surrender, Norman of Torn?" cried De Montfort.

"Yes," was the reply, "when this floor be ankle deep in English blood and my heart has ceased to beat; then will I surrender."

"Come, come," cried the King. "Let your men take the dog, De Montfort!"

"Have at him, then," ordered the Earl, turning toward

the waiting men-at-arms, none of whom seemed overly anxious to advance upon the doomed outlaw.

But an officer of the guard set them the example, and so they pushed forward in a body toward Norman of Torn; twenty blades bared against one.

There was no play now for the Outlaw of Torn; it was grim battle and his only hope that he might take a fearful toll of his enemies before he himself went down.

And so he fought as he never fought before, to kill as many and as quickly as he might. And to those who watched it was as though the young officer of the Guard had not come within reach of that terrible blade ere he lay dead upon the floor, and then the point of death passed into the lungs of one of the men-at-arms, scarcely pausing ere it pierced the heart of a third.

The soldiers fell back momentarily, awed by the frightful havoc of that mighty arm. Before De Montfort could urge them on to renew the attack a girlish figure clothed in a long riding cloak burst through the little knot of men as they stood facing their lone antagonist.

With a low cry of mingled rage and indignation Bertrade de Montfort threw herself before the Devil of Torn, and facing the astonished company of king, prince, nobles and soldiers drew herself to her full height, and with all the pride of race and blood that was her right of heritage from a French king on her father's side and an English king on her mother's, she flashed her defiance and contempt in the single word:

"Cowards!"

"What means this, girl?" demanded De Montfort. "Art gone stark mad? Know thou that this fellow be the Outlaw of Torn?"

"If I had not before known it, My Lord," she replied haughtily, "it would be plain to me now as I see forty cowards hesitating to attack a lone man. What other man in all England could stand thus against forty? A lion at bay with forty jackals yelping at his feet."

"Enough, girl," cried the King, "what be this knave to thee?"

"He loves me, Your Majesty," she replied proudly, "and I, him."

"Thou lov'st this low born cut-throat, Bertrade," cried Henry. "Thou, a De Montfort, the daughter of my sister; who have seen this muderer's accursed mark upon the foreheads of thy kin; thou have seen him flaunt his defiance in the King's, thy uncle's, face, and bend his whole life to preying upon thy people; thou lov'st this monster?"

"I love him, My Lord King."

"Thou lov'st him, Bertrade?" asked Philip of France in a low tone, pressing nearer to the girl.

"Yes, Philip," she said, a little note of sadness and finality in her voice; but her eyes met his squarely and bravely.

Instantly the sword of the young Prince leaped from its scabbard, and facing De Montfort and the others he backed to the side of Norman of Torn.

"That she loves him be enough for me to know, my gentlemen," he said. "Who takes the man Bertrade de Montfort loves must take Philip of France as well."

Norman of Torn laid his left hand upon the other's shoulder.

"No, thou must not do this thing, my friend," he said. "It be my fight and I will fight it alone. Go, I beg of thee, and take her with thee, out of harm's way."

As they argued Simon de Montfort and the King had spoken together, and at a word from the former the soldiers rushed suddenly to the attack again. It was a cowardly strategem, for they knew that the two could not fight with the girl between them and their adversaries. And thus, by weight of numbers, they took Bertrade de Montfort and the Prince away from Norman of Torn without a blow being struck, and then the little, grim, gray, old man stepped forward.

"There be but one sword in all England, nay in all the world that can, alone, take Norman of Torn," he said, addressing the King, "and that sword be mine; keep thy cattle back, out of my way." And, without waiting for a reply, the grim, gray man sprang in to engage him whom for twenty years he had called son.

Norman of Torn came out of his corner to meet his new-found enemy, and there, in the apartment of the Queen of England in the castle of Battel, was fought such a duel as no man there had ever seen before, nor is it credible that its like was ever fought before or since.

The world's two greatest swordsmen: teacher and pupil—the one with the strength of a young bull, the other with the cunning of an old gray fox; and both with a lifetime of training behind them, and the lust of blood and hate before them—thrust and parried and cut until those that gazed awestricken upon the marvellous sword play scarcely breathed in the tensity of their wonder.

Back and forth about the room they moved, while those who had come to kill pressed back to make room for the contestants. Now was the young man forcing his older foeman more and more upon the defensive. Slowly, but as sure as death, he was winning ever nearer and nearer to victory. The old man saw it too. He had devoted years of his life to training that mighty sword arm that it might deal out death to others, and now; ah! the grim justice of the retribution, he at last was to fall before its diabolical cunning.

He could not win in fair fight against Norman of Torn; that the wily Frenchman saw; but now that death was so close upon him that he felt its cold breath condensing on his brow, he had no stomach to die, and so he cast about for any means whereby he might escape the result of his rash venture.

Presently he saw his opportunity. Norman of Torn stood beside the body of one of his earlier antagonists. Slowly the old man worked around until the body lay directly behind the outlaw, and then with a final rally and one great last burst of supreme swordsmanship, he rushed Norman of Torn back for a bare step—it was enough; the outlaw's foot struck the prostrate corpse; he staggered, and for one brief instant his sword arm rose, ever so little, as he strove to retain his equilibrium; but that little was enough, it was what the gray old snake had expected, and he was ready. Like lightning his sword shot through the opening, and, for the first time in his life of continual combat and death, Norman of Torn felt cold steel tear his flesh. But ere he fell his sword responded to the last fierce command of that iron will, and as his body sank limply to the floor, rolling with outstretched arms, upon its back, the little, grim, gray man went down also, clutching frantically at a gleaming blade buried in his chest.

For an instant the watchers stood as though petrified, and then Bertrade de Montfort, tearing herself from the restraining hand of her father, rushed to the side of the lifeless body of the man she loved. Kneeling there beside him she called his name aloud, as she unlaced his helm. Tearing the steel headgear from him she caressed his face, kissing the white forehead and the still lips.

"Oh God! Oh God!" she murmured. "Why hast thou taken him? Outlaw though he was, in his little finger was more of honor, of chivalry, of true manhood than courses through the veins of all the nobles of England.

"I do not wonder that he preyed upon you," she cried, turning upon the knights behind her. "His life was clean, thine be rotten; he was loyal to his friends and to the downtrodden, ye be traitors at heart, all; and ever be ye trampling upon those who be down that they may sink deeper into the mud. *Mon Dieu!* How I hate you," she finished. And as she spoke the words Bertrade de Montfort looked straight into the eyes of her father.

The old Earl turned his head, for at heart he was a brave, broad, kindly man, and he regretted what he had done in the haste and heat of anger.

"Come, child," said the King, "thou art distraught; thou sayest what thou mean not. The world is better that this man be dead. He was an enemy of organized society, he preyed ever upon his fellows. Life in England will be safer after this day. Do not weep over the clay of a nameless adventurer who knew not his own father."

Some one had lifted the little, grim, gray, old man to a sitting posture. He was not dead. Occasionally he coughed, and when he did his frame was racked with suffering, and blood flowed from his mouth and nostrils.

At last they saw that he was trying to speak. Weakly he motioned toward the King. Henry came toward him.

"Thou hast won thy sovereign's gratitude, my man," said the King, kindly. "What be thy name?"

The old fellow tried to speak, but the effort brought on another paroxysm of coughing. At last he managed to whisper.

"Look—at—me. Dost thou—not—remember me? The —foils—the—blow—twenty—long—years. Thou—spat—upon —me."

Henry knelt and peered into the dying face.

"De Vac!" he exclaimed.

The old man nodded. Then he pointed to where lay Norman of Torn.

"Outlaw — highwayman — scourge — of — England. Look—upon—his—face. Open—his tunic—left—breast."

He stopped from very weakness, and then in another moment, with a final effort: "De—Vac's—revenge. God—

damn—the—English," and slipped forward upon the rushes, dead.

The King had heard, and De Montfort and the Queen. They stood looking into each other's eyes with a strange fixity, for what seemed an eternity, before any dared to move; and then, as though they feared what they should see, they bent over the form of the Outlaw of Torn for the first time.

The Queen gave a little cry as she saw the still, quiet face turned up to hers.

"Edward!" she whispered.

"Not Edward, Madame," said De Montfort, "but—"

The King knelt beside the still form, across the breast of which lay the unconscious body of Bertrade de Montfort. Gently he lifted her to the waiting arms of Philip of France, and then the King with his own hands tore off the shirt of mail, and with trembling fingers ripped wide the tunic where it covered the left breast of the Devil of Torn.

"Oh God!" he cried, and buried his head in his arms.

The Queen had seen also, and with a little moan she sank beside the body of her second born, crying out

"Oh Richard, my boy, my boy!" And as she bent still lower to kiss the lily mark upon the left breast of the son she had not seen to know for over twenty years, she paused, and with frantic haste she pressed her ear to his breast.

"He lives!" she almost shrieked. "Quick, Henry, our son lives!"

Bertrade de Montfort had regained consciousness almost before Philip of France had raised her from the floor, and she stood now, leaning on his arm, watching with wide, questioning eyes the strange scene being enacted at her feet.

Slowly the lids of Norman of Torn lifted with returning consciousness. Before him, on her knees in the blood spattered rushes of the floor, knelt Eleanor, Queen of England, alternately chafing and kissing his hands.

A sore wound indeed to have brought on such a wild delirium, thought the Outlaw of Torn.

He felt his body, in a half sitting, half reclining position, resting against one who knelt behind him, and as he lifted his head to see whom it might be supporting him he looked into the eyes of the King, upon whose breast his head rested.

Strange vagaries of a disordered brain! Yes it must have been a very terrible wound that the little old man of Torn had given him; but why could he not dream that Bertrade de Montfort held him? And then his eyes wandered about among the throng of ladies, nobles and soldiers standing uncovered and with bowed heads about him. Presently he found her.

"Bertrade!" he whispered.

The girl came and knelt beside him, opposite the Queen.

"Bertrade, tell me thou art real; that thou at least be no dream."

"I be very real, dear heart," she answered, "and these others be real, also. When thou art stronger, thou shalt understand the strange thing that has happened. These who wert thine enemies, Norman of Torn, be thy best friends now—that thou should know so that thou may rest in peace until thou be better."

He groped for her hand, and, finding it, closed his eyes with a faint sigh.

They bore him to a cot in an apartment next the Queen's, and all that night the mother and the promised wife of the Outlaw of Torn sat bathing his fevered forehead. The King's chirurgeon was there also, while the King and De Montfort paced the corridor without.

And it is ever thus; whether in hovel or palace; in the days of Moses, or in the days that be ours; the lamb that has been lost and is found again be always the best beloved.

Toward morning Norman of Torn fell into a quiet and natural sleep; the fever and delirium had succumbed before his perfect health and iron constitution. The chirurgeon turned to the Queen and Bertrade de Montfort.

"You had best retire, ladies," he said, "and rest; the Prince will live."

Late that afternoon he awoke, and no amount of persuasion or commands on the part of the King's chirurgeon could restrain him from arising.

"I beseech thee to lie quiet, My Lord Prince," urged the chirurgeon.

"Why call thou me prince?" asked Norman of Torn.

"There be one without whose right it be to explain that to thee," replied the chirurgeon, "and when thou be clothed, if rise thou wilt, thou mayst see her, My Lord."

The chirurgeon aided him to dress, and, opening the

door, he spoke to a sentry who stood just without. The sentry transmitted the message to a young squire who was waiting there, and presently the door was thrown open again from without, and a voice announced:

"Her Majesty, the Queen!"

Norman of Torn looked up in unfeigned surprise, and then there came back to him the scene in the Queen's apartment the night before. It was all a sore perplexity to him; he could not fathom it, nor did he attempt to.

And now, as in a dream, he saw the Queen of England coming toward him across the small room, her arms outstretched; her beautiful face radiant with happiness and love.

"Richard, my son!" exclaimed Eleanor, coming to him and taking his face in her hands and kissing him.

"Madame!" exclaimed the surprised man. "Be all the world gone crazy?"

And then she told him the strange story of the little lost prince of England.

When she had finished, he knelt at her feet, taking her hand in his and raising it to his lips.

"I did not know, Madame," he said, "or never would my sword have been bared in other service than thine. If thou canst forgive me, Madame, never can I forgive myself."

"Take it not so hard, my son," said Eleanor of England, "it be no fault of thine, and there be nothing to forgive; only happiness and rejoicing should we feel, now that thou be found again."

"Forgiveness!" said a man's voice behind them. "Forsooth, it be we that should ask forgiveness; hunting down our own son with swords and halters.

"Any but a fool might have known that it was no base born knave who sent the King's army back, naked to the King, and rammed the King's message down his messenger's throat.

"By all the saints, Richard, thou be every inch a King's son, an' though we made sour faces at the time, we be all the prouder of thee now."

The Queen and the outlaw had turned at the first words to see the King standing behind them, and now Norman of Torn rose, half smiling, and greeted his father.

"They be sorry jokes, Sire," he said. "Methinks it had been better had Richard remained lost. It will do the honor of the Plantagenets but little good to acknowledge the Outlaw of Torn as a prince of the blood."

But they would not have it so, and it remained for a later King of England to wipe the great name from the pages of history—perhaps a jealous king.

Presently the King and Queen, adding their pleas to those of the chirurgeon, prevailed upon him to lie down once more, and when he had done so they left him, that he might sleep again; but no sooner had the door closed behind them than he arose and left the apartment by another exit.

It was by chance that, in a deep set window, he found her for whom he was searching. She sat looking wistfully into space, an expression half sad upon her beautiful face. She did not see him as he approached, and he stood there for several moments watching her dear profile, and the rising and falling of her bosom over that true and loyal heart that had beaten so proudly against all the power of a mighty throne for the despised Outlaw of Torn.

He did not speak, but presently that strange, subtile sixth sense which warns us that we are not alone, though our eyes see not nor our ears hear, caused her to turn.

With a little cry she arose, and then, curtsying low after the manner of the court, said:

"What would My Lord Richard, Prince of England, of his poor subject?" And then, more gravely, "My Lord, I have been raised at court, and I understand that a prince does not wed rashly, and so let us forget what passed between Bertrade de Montfort and Norman of Torn."

"Prince Richard of England will in no wise disturb royal precedents," he replied, "for he will wed not rashly, but most wisely, since he will wed none but Bertrade de Montfort." And he who had been the Outlaw of Torn took the fair young girl in his arms, adding: "If she still loves me, now that I be a prince?"

She put her arms about his neck, and drew his cheek down close to hers.

"It was not the outlaw that I loved, Richard, nor be it the prince I love now; it be all the same to me, prince or highwayman—it be thee I love, dear heart—just thee."

EDGAR RICE BURROUGHS

$1.50 each

Beyond the Farthest Star

Cave Girl

The Deputy Sheriff of
Comanche County

Eternal Savage

I am a Barbarian

The Lad And The Lion

The Land of Hidden Men

The Lost Continent

The Mad King

Monster Men

Moon Maid

The Moon Men

The Mucker

The Oakdale Affair

Outlaw of Torn

Return Of The Mucker

The Rider